A PERFECT STUDY

"I fear we share little common ground, Lord Devlin. And what little we may have you do your best to shovel away."

"At least we could agree on some things." He stepped toward her, smiling.

"And what are they?" Jane asked, wary yet intrigued.

"For example," he went on, "we could agree that your eyes are green. And a most delightful shade of green, I might add."

"No," she told him even as she felt a spark of pleasure on hearing his compliment. "My eyes happen to be hazel."

"But your hair, surely your hair is red. And a glorious shade of red."

"My hair happens to be auburn." She held up her hand before he could go on, reminding herself she had no interest in Lord Devlin as a man despite the unexpected glow his words brought. Probably her interest in him, merely an interest, she reminded herself, not a fascination, came about because he was perhaps a perfect specimen of a breed she had little knowledge of and little use for—the English aristocratic gentleman. Lord Devlin offered her the opportunity to study one at first hand. . . .

ZEBRA REGENCIES
ARE
THE TALK OF THE TON!

Lord Devlin's Dilemma

Olivia Sumner

ZEBRA BOOKS
KENSINGTON PUBLISHING CORP.

ZEBRA BOOKS are published by

Kensington Publishing Corp.
850 Third Avenue
New York, NY 10022

Zebra and the Z logo Reg. U.S. Pat. & TM Off.

First Printing: February, 1995

Printed in the United States of America

One

After adding the long column of figures and writing the discouraging result on the bottommost line of her estate ledger, Jane Sterling put down her pen and shook her head in despair.

"Completely impossible," she said. "I have no alternative, I must sell Lyon Hall."

Chatter, her black cat, raised his head and looked a question at his mistress from his perch on a cushion atop one of the chairs near the fireplace.

"You should be overjoyed to hear we must return to New Orleans," Jane told him, "since you find England so very inhospitable."

As though agreeing, the cat inclined his head, once again closing his eyes and nestling into the pillow. Beyond him, wind-driven rain slashed across the window panes while outside Lyon Hall the night was every bit as black as Chatter's fur.

Sighing, Jane pushed the ledger away. There *must* be a way to save Lyon Hall, she told herself, there must be something she could do. Lulled by the ticking of the Tompion clock on the mantel and the crackling of the dying embers in the fireplace, she closed her eyes, drooping with fatigue. Rousing almost at once, she shook her head violently. No! She refused to allow herself to surrender to the comfort of sleep.

Looking around the sparsely furnished drawing room, she realized she had not only become accustomed to Lyon Hall but had grown fond of the crumbling mansion despite the country house's isolation, despite its disrepair after years of neglect, despite its drafts and drab dinginess. Lyon Hall was hers; she had come to love the hopeless old place, to consider it her home.

She had never had a real home since early childhood.

The clock chimed one; the single candle on the writing desk—her dire financial straits had forced her to pinch not only pounds but pennies as well—flickered as it burned low in its socket; the glowing embers in the grate did little to alleviate the creeping chill or to help dispel the encompassing gloom. Unnoticed, the dark of the night seemed to have crept into the room where now it lurked in the shadowed corners.

Let the fire go out, she told herself dispiritedly, let the candle gutter. What did it matter if she was left in the cold without light? After six months at Lyon Hall she could easily find her way from room to room in the dark.

"I will not have it!" Jane stood suddenly, sending her chair thudding down to the threadbare carpet behind her. Chatter's head jerked up in alarm, his yellow eyes glinting.

Snatching the candle from the desk, Jane hurried to

the hearth, lighting the twin candles on the mantel. After laying two more small logs on the dying fire, she crossed and recrossed the room, first lighting the candles in the sconces on the wall, then lowering the chandelier and setting all of its candles ablaze before raising it again. She placed a small, glowing candelabra in each of the four windows even though she realized no one in this isolated corner of West Sussex was likely to be abroad at this hour to witness her gesture of defiance.

Chatter had watched her progress around the room with interest though seemingly without surprise. After Jane returned the candle to the desk and was leaning over to right the overturned chair, however, the cat leaped to the floor and, facing the windows at the front of the house, arched his back and hissed.

"Whatever is the matter?" Jane asked him, leaving the chair where it lay and walking toward the cat with her hand outstretched, intending to comfort him.

Ignoring her, Chatter spun about and fled through the archway into the parlor that she had renamed the King's Room. Open-mouthed, Jane stared after him, trying to recall when she had seen Chatter this upset.

A loud knocking echoed through the house. Once, twice, three times. Jane drew in her breath in a startled gasp.

The knocking, three reverberating clangs of metal on metal, came again. Someone was at the door, the front door. Who could it possibly be so late at night? Would Hendricks answer? No, he had long since retired to his upstairs room.

After a brief hesitation, Jane walked along the entry hall to the front door where she paused once more before sliding the bolt free. She opened the door a crack. As she peered into the darkness, breathing in the dampness of the October night, she heard the steady tapping of rain on the graveled sweep of the drive.

" 'Tis Lord Devlin," came a man's husky voice sounding as though he announced the arrival of royalty, "seeking lodging for the night."

Only when she eased the door a few inches wider did she discern the speaker, a squat dark figure almost indistinguishable from the surrounding night, water sluicing from the turned-down brim of his hat. "Are you Lord Devlin?" she asked.

Before the stranger could answer, a tall figure appeared from out of the gloom. "No," he told her, "*I* am Lord Devlin."

Even though he had uttered only five words and those in an accent alien to her American ears, Jane had the immediate impression that here was a gentleman of the *ton.* An English gentleman, she had read, was by definition a man not required to work for a living.

She heard a scrabbling on the gravel and a moment later a four-footed form appeared at Lord Devlin's feet. Sharp barks startled her and she stepped back.

"Horatio! Quiet!" The dog subsided at Lord Devlin's command.

Horatio explained Chatter's flight, Jane thought. The cat must have heard or sensed the presence of the dog.

"Be so kind as to inform your master without delay," Lord Devlin told Jane, "that Lord Devlin's carriage has suffered an unfortunate and quite unexpected mishap on the Midhurst Road, forcing him to beg refuge for the night."

Beg refuge? she echoed to herself. I doubt if you were ever forced to beg for anything in your life, my good Lord Devlin.

"Without delay," Lord Devlin repeated.

"I happen to have no master," she told him.

Unable to see his expression in the dark, she imagined him scowling down at her. Before he could reply, she said, "My name is Jane Sterling and I am mistress of Lyon Hall." She swung the door wide and stepped to one side. "Please come in, Lord Devlin. And you, too, sir," she said to the stocky man standing deferentially behind Lord Devlin.

"Capital!" Devlin said. "Cunningham will tend to Horatio and the horses," he added, nodding brusquely to Jane as he entered the hall. After unbuttoning his greatcoat, he waited as though expecting someone to take it from him. When no one did he shrugged it off and tossed the many-caped coat onto a chair before turning to peer into the shadowed recesses of the hall.

"This way, my lord," she said, wondering if he noted the tinge of mock deference in her voice. She led him along the hall while he murmured perfunctory thanks— "splendid of you, most grateful"—ushering him into the drawing room and smiling when she saw him blink in astonishment at the blinding display of lighted candles. He strode to the hearth, his hands held toward the fireplace where tongues of flame had begun licking around the sides of the new logs in the grate.

"I saw the lights in the windows," he said, turning to her. "I saw—"

He stopped, really looking at her for the first time, staring at her with his dark brown eyes, eyes the color of chestnuts. At first his face showed surprise, as though he recognized her from somewhere, then admiration, but finally he frowned.

Surprisingly, he wore no hat; his black hair was wet from the rain and drops of water glistened on his angular face. Also surprisingly, he seemed impeccably groomed for a gentleman traveling after midnight who had suffered a mishap on the road. He wore a grey waistcoat and a carelessly tied red cravat; only his mud-streaked black boots marred his fashionable appearance. He was at least thirty, she guessed, some ten years older than she.

Jane drew in a deep breath as she tried to collect her suddenly scattered thoughts. There was something about this Lord Devlin that seemed to muddle her usually clear thoughts. Though confused, she somehow sensed she had come to an abrupt turning in her life. She tingled with what she decided was either eager anticipation or a foreboding, just as she had a year ago in the office of M. Maurice Lusignon at number 61 rue de St. Louis. She still remembered not only the lawyer's address but the lingering scent of tobacco in the room and the faint peal of the cathedral bells in the distance.

"A distant cousin of yours," M. Lusignon had informed her, "a Mr. Richard Lyon of Lyon Hall, in the English county of Sussex, has gone to his reward and bequeathed his estate to you, Mlle. Sterling, his only direct and surviving heir. I believe a relative by marriage, a Miss Estelle Winward, spinster, is presently residing at the Hall. I shall, if you wish, write to Mr. Lyon's solicitors"—his finger tapped the letter on his desk—"requesting them to arrange for the sale of Lyon Hall, suggesting they consider conducting an auction to dispose of the property."

Without thinking, acting solely on impulse as she so often did, Jane shook her head. Repeating M. Lusignon's words to herself—Lyon Hall, Sussex, England, she pictured stone towers, a sweep of lawn, servants in livery. No, she would not agree to sell the estate before she had even seen it, instead she would journey to England, she would ask Estelle Winward to stay on at Lyon Hall, she would start a new life in the land of her forefathers. . . .

She blinked and the memory vanished. A frowning Lord Devlin, she discovered, was still staring at her. She looked down at her white muslin afternoon dress, worried she might have spotted it with ink but found nothing amiss. Touching her auburn ringlets, she glanced past him at the looking glass but saw only the reflection of a portrait of one of her Lyon ancestors.

Lord Devlin's gaze left her, returned, then left her once more. As he had in the entry hall, he peered carefully around the room before shaking his head as though in disappointment. It was almost as though he was seeking something, something he did not find.

"I had the misfortune," he told her, "to have one of the rear wheels of my landau quite unexpectedly detach itself from the axle, almost causing my carriage—a landau I purchased no more than eight months ago, I might add—to overturn. When I happened to look between the two pillars crowned by the stone lions guarding the entrance to the Hall, I saw the lights in the windows through the trees."

Fate had brought him here, Jane told herself, fate had loosened the wheel on his carriage, fate had prompted her to place the candelabras in the windows. Not chance—fate. Chance was random, a matter of coincidence, while there was a purpose to fate. What that purpose was in this case she did not know. Hope momentarily lifted her heart. Improbable though it seemed, was it possible that Lord Devlin had been sent here to save Lyon Hall?

"I was working late," she told him, gesturing toward the ledger on the desk. She deliberately refrained from addressing him as "my lord."

"You were balancing the estate books?" As he righted the fallen chair with a quick, easy sweep of his arm, he glanced at her. "Surely you must employ a land agent?"

"If Lyon Hall produced enough income, no doubt I *would* hire a land agent. And have the roof replaced where it leaks. And have all the chimneys swept. And do a thousand other things that need doing."

His raised eyebrows told her he was both dumbfounded and disapproving. "Miss Sterling," he said sternly, "one never admits to one's funds being at low ebb. An English gentleman may be hopelessly in debt with the cent percenters hounding him relentlessly, he may be planning to flee to Calais before tomorrow's dawn, but still he dons his best evening attire and spends his final night in London, perhaps the last night he will ever spend in England, at Almack's or White's or whatever his favorite haunt might be. All with never so much as a word of complaint or regret or the slightest hint of his exquisite distress. I suggest, Miss Sterling, that you do the same."

"I have no desire whatsoever to emulate impoverished English gentlemen. I have no desire to heroically sink beneath the mountainous waves of debt with all my flags flying and all my cannon firing."

Lord Devlin raised an eyebrow and smiled crookedly, at the same time spreading out his arms in a gesture that encompassed the entire drawing room. "And yet you appear to be welcoming your sorry fate," he said, "with every light blazing."

She bit back a denial when she realized he was right. That had been precisely what she had been doing when she lit the candles. Lord Devlin was more perceptive than she'd suspected.

"Although I believe in making the best of hardship," she said at last, "I would never choose deceit over the truth. Lyon Hall does not pay its way and I admit it."

"Is this policy of truth at all costs a peculiar colonial virtue of some sort? I say colonial because I detect a foreign strain in your voice, something a less kind person might describe as a slight nasal quality. Are you Australian? Or Canadian?"

Lord Devlin was the one with the accent, she reminded herself, so much so that at times she had difficulty understanding what he was saying; she, on the other hand, had no accent whatsoever. "I happen to be an American," she told him proudly. "From the city of New Orleans in the United States of America."

About to go on, she paused. Her father had been a sea captain sailing out of Boston when he married Marie La Branche, a seventeen-year-old French girl from New Orleans. Jane had no memory of the mother who had died at her birth; her father had gone down with all hands on the *Anna Celeste* during a hurricane in the Caribbean in the fall of 1812. But she said nothing: her family history was no concern of Lord Devlin's.

"Ah, just so, an American," he said. "That fact explains a great deal. Greeting unexpected visitors at your front door at one in the morning is probably an American—" He shook his head. "Pray pardon me, my dear Miss Sterling," he said, "I forget myself. For some reason, you succeed in bringing forth the worst in me, the very worst. Our two countries may find themselves at war but I hope we two will remain at peace."

"I fear we share little common ground, Lord Devlin. And what little we may have you do your best to shovel away."

"At least we could agree on some things." He stepped toward her, smiling.

"And what are they?" she asked, wary yet intrigued.

"For example," he went on, "we could agree that

your eyes are green. And a most delightful shade of green, I might add."

"No," she told him even as she felt a spark of pleasure on hearing his compliment. "My eyes happen to be hazel."

"But your hair, surely your hair is red. And a glorious shade of red."

"My hair happens to be auburn." She held up her hand before he could go on, reminding herself she had no interest in Lord Devlin as a man despite the unexpected glow his words brought. Probably her interest in him, merely an interest, she reminded herself, not a fascination, came about because he was perhaps a perfect specimen of a breed she had little knowledge of and little use for—the English aristocratic gentleman. Lord Devlin offered her the opportunity to study one at first hand.

"The hour is late," she said. "I do believe we could agree on this: the time has long since passed for me to show you to your bed chamber."

Lord Devlin bowed slightly. "Quite right," he admitted.

When she lifted the extinguisher from its hook at the side of the fireplace, he took it from her and walked around the room snuffing out the candles. Lifting a still-lighted candelabra from in front of one of the windows, he started to rejoin her when he halted in mid-stride, raising the light in the direction of the archway leading to the King's Room.

"What is it?" she asked.

"I believe I espy the gleam of a cat's eyes coming from the darkness."

Following his nod, she saw the glint of Chatter's yellow eyes. Behind the cat, the candlelight reflected from a glass case.

Lord Devlin strode into the King's Room, stopping to stare at the case and its contents as Chatter scurried across the room and leaped onto a chair. When Jane walked to the archway, the cat looked first at Lord Devlin and then at her. Who is this strange gentleman, the cat seemed to be asking her, who holds a candelabra aloft as he slowly circles the case sitting in the center of the room?

The display case, with panes of glass on all four sides, sat in proud isolation on a wooden pedestal. Inside, draped on a wooden tailor's dummy, was a gentleman's blue velvet cloak fastened at the throat by a chain of gold. The dull color and evident stiffness of the cloth spoke of great age; the richness of the material spoke of quality; the jagged tears in the fabric spoke of hard use.

When at last Lord Devlin turned to Jane, he asked, "Is this a family heirloom?"

She nodded. "The King's Cloak has been in the Lyon family for at least a hundred years. When I came to Lyon Hall six months ago I found the cloak displayed just as you see it now."

"The King's Cloak," he repeated, "that does have a ring to it. And what king might that have been?"

Though his tone seemed to show mere idle curiosity, Jane could tell by his rapt attention that Lord Devlin was more than casually interested in her answer. How strange, she thought. Was it possible he had heard of the cloak? She had understood that the ancient garment, though highly valued by the Lyon family, had become something of an object of ridicule in Midhurst and other nearby villages. "The Lyon Folly," some called it, suggesting the cloak was a hoax of some sort.

"The king may have been Charles I or Charles II," she said. "From what I was told, no one in the family, at least in recent years seemed to be quite certain. Or perhaps this isn't a king's cloak at all since some of the family records refer to Oliver Cromwell in connection with the cloak. More likely, this is merely a very old but completely ordinary cloak and these stories of kings are merely tales woven from whole cloth." Aunt Estelle, Jane recalled, had had no notion of the origin of the cloak. And had shown little interest.

"Charles I or Charles II." Lord Devlin nodded as he echoed her words, almost, Jane thought, in triumph. "Would it be possible," he asked, "for me to touch this garment that might have once been worn by no less than a king of England?"

"Of course." Jane stepped forward and unlatched the door of the case. "I never have been able to find a key," she said.

Lord Devlin reached inside the case and reverently ran his hand from the shoulder of the cloak down to its lower hem in a gesture resembling a caress. Finally he stepped back, his gaze still on the cloak, and reluctantly closed and latched the glass door.

"This particular cloak is hardly unique," Jane said. "In fact, I discovered two others much like it in one of the Hall's attic storerooms."

"If you were English rather than American and so were aware of the grandeur of the history of our monarchy over not a mere forty years—1776 is the year of the beginning of your country's so-called declaration of independence, I believe—but ever since 800 A.D., you might be able to begin to appreciate the significance of the cloak as much as I do."

"I am aware of a bit of your history," she said, stung by what she considered his hauteur, "though how grand that history was is surely a matter of opinion. The two kings who might have owned the cloak were both Stuarts, I believe. Charles I was overthrown by Oliver Cromwell more than a hundred and fifty years ago and had the misfortune to be beheaded. His son fled to France, much like the impoverished gentleman you mentioned, and returned ten or fifteen years later after Cromwell died. He became Charles II who, or so I read somewhere, never said a foolish thing and never did a wise one."

"Yes, you have the gist of it," Lord Devlin admitted, albeit grudgingly, "though I might disagree with your low opinion of Charles II."

"I might mention that I am also aware that your present king is mad."

"Men might be fallible but our monarchy has lasted a thousand years and will last at least another thousand. 'The king is dead, long live the king.' Our King George III will be remembered long after the leaders of your rebellious country, that vast wilderness you call the United States, are forgotten."

She pictured the portraits she had seen of the first four presidents: George Washington, John Adams, Thomas Jefferson, and the president now in his second term, James Madison. Could Lord Devlin be right? She sincerely doubted so, but she held her tongue.

"The hour *is* late," he said, retrieving the candelabra from the top of the glass case.

Nodding, she took the candelabra from him and started into the drawing room only to have Lord Devlin pause and glance back for a last glimpse of the King's Cloak before following her along the hall to the sweep of the stairs and up to the corridor leading to the bed chambers on the first floor.

"My luggage?" he asked when she opened the door to his room. "Cunningham will have fetched it from the carriage by now."

"Joshua, the stableboy, will show Mr. Cunningham the way to your chamber," she told him. "He knows this is the only room we keep ready for guests."

Lord Devlin bowed and, for a moment, she thought he was about to take her hand and raise it to his lips. Her breath caught at the prospect but he merely smiled and retreated into his chamber. When he closed the door behind him, he left her surprised at the depth of her disappointment.

Jane stood staring at the closed door. So much for his admiring glances, so much for your "delightful eyes" and "glorious hair," she told herself ruefully. It had been painfully evident that Lord Devlin had a much greater interest in a torn and tattered cloak than he did in Jane Sterling.

Two

Charles Worthington, Earl of Devlin, woke to find sunlight slanting across his bed chamber. Had he overslept? He reached to the night table and held up his pocket watch. Twenty minutes after eight. Damn, so much for his good intentions, so much for his vow to be out of bed and doing by seven at the latest.

Devlin sat up, frowning, finding that his dream still lingered in his mind. . . .

He was sitting in absolute darkness, waiting for he knew not what. Suddenly a light appeared in the far distance, a burning taper held by a woman in a diaphanous white gown. Although her face was indistinct, he somehow knew who she was: Jane Sterling. As she slowly approached him, she reached first to her right and then to her left with the taper, lighting one candle after another, each taller than the last, until an aisle of lights sparkled like precious gems behind her.

Jane stopped at the foot of the low steps leading to where he sat on what he now realized was his throne, knelt and bowed her head in obeisance. He rose and walked down toward her. How tiny she seemed, how defenseless, how appealing, how desirable.

When he stood directly above her he extended his left hand, nodding in satisfaction as she took his hand in hers and kissed his signet ring. While she still held his fingers to her warm lips, he placed his other hand lightly on the softness of her golden hair.

A voice from the shadows whispered, "The King's Cloak, the King's Cloak."

Forgetting all else, he glanced around him but saw nothing. "Where?" he demanded.

As though in answer, one by one the candles blinked out and in a matter of seconds he was again in total darkness. A sudden gust of wind chilled him, rain swept down on him and he shuddered not so much from the cold but from the knowledge that Jane was gone. Where was she?

He groped in front of him but his hands found nothing but emptiness. He raised his head and cried out in hopeless despair.

At that moment he had wakened. Now he sat on the edge of the bed, his hand to his chin as he pondered the meaning of his dream, for he had always believed these phantoms of the night carried hidden messages. Many centuries before, Joseph had listened to the pharaoh recounting his dream and accurately predicted seven prosperous years for the land of Egypt followed by seven years of famine. If only he had the powers of a Joseph.

His dream must be a warning, Devlin decided. Miss Jane Sterling might appear innocent and defenseless but he knew appearances were often deceiving, especially where beautiful women were concerned. Beware! Be awake on every suit. No matter how beguiling he found her green eyes and glorious hair, he had to be on his guard or she would deceive him, lead him astray, divert him from his duty.

Beautiful? Why had he thought of her as beautiful? Jane Sterling was a fetching miss, perhaps, more attractive than most, certainly, and possessing a hint of a spirit that challenged him. But hardly beautiful. And that out-of-fashion white muslin gown she wore last night. How dreadful. And her American accent, the sound akin to a fingernail on slate. How grating. And her opinions of George III and England, his king and his country. How abominable.

And yet.

He rubbed his chest as he recalled their meeting. When he had first looked at Jane Sterling, really looked at her, he had felt a strange pain deep within himself, as though the hand of God had reached inside him and violently twisted his heart.

Such a strange and singular sensation! But, he reminded himself, after giving the matter a little thought he had arrived at a simple enough explanation. Though he had felt nothing amiss at the time, he must have twisted a muscle in his chest while helping Cunningham with that damned carriage wheel.

Forewarned by his disturbing dream, he would do his best to avoid Miss Jane Sterling during the remainder of the day. And then tonight, while the house slept, he would do what he had to do. . . .

An older woman was seated at the table when Lord Devlin entered the breakfast room, a thin-faced woman with grey hair pulled tightly into a bun at the back of her head. Despite himself, he felt a sharp twinge of disappointment at not finding Miss Sterling at breakfast. Are you becoming addled? he demanded of himself. After deciding to avoid her, why in the name of heaven are you disappointed not to find her at breakfast?

"Miss Estelle Winward, your humble servant," the grey-haired woman said after Devlin introduced himself. As soon as he was seated across from her, she went on, "How honored Lyon Hall is to have you here, Lord Devlin, even though our pride in your presence must be mingled with our condolences that only an unfortunate accident brought you to seek succor on our doorstep, as it were."

Devlin nodded without attempting to untangle Miss Winward's sentiment.

"How like the old days," she went on, "when Mr. Henry Lyon was in the first blush of his youth and the Hall was filled to overflowing with his guests even though some may not have been all they should have been. *Tempus fugit,* as they say, but not always in the manner we might choose for if wishes were horses, beggars might ride. Not that Jane fails to do her best, she's a lovely girl, and I must tell you she has been kindness itself to me, but—" She paused.

Devlin leaned forward at the mention of his hostess's name. "But—?" he encouraged as an old gentleman in faded livery began to serve his breakfast.

Estelle waited until they were alone before answering. "Unfortunately for the dear child," she said in a low voice, "no matter how diligently one tries, if one happens not to be English *and* one has more than a touch of French blood besides *and* one is not to the manner born, well . . . I think I need say no more, my lord."

So Jane Sterling had French antecedents. He frowned. France had been the haven of Charles II during the Cromwell years. Was it possible Miss Sterling knew more about the King's Cloak than she admitted?

"Is Miss Sterling about this morning?" he inquired.

"Oh, yes, up and about and out of the house. She rides every morning, rain or shine or come what may. Evidently she enjoys living here in the country. As for myself, I was London born and bred but, alas, alas, early on I was forced to leave town for Sussex but my heart is in London as I feel certain, my lord, yours is as well. Duty, perforce, has its demands and we must, as good Christians, make the best of our lot in life, no matter how sorry. Mr. Henry Lyon refused to accept no for an answer, he insisted I come to help with little Georgiana and, after the poor dear child passed over, I stayed on."

Devlin tried to keep his mind from wandering. "I find equal pleasure in London and the country," he told her.

"Your sentiments do you honor, my lord, but when one is forced to live all twelve months of the year in rural surroundings and, to make matters worse, in this drear tag end of Sussex, one finds one's patience tried by the endless round of—" Estelle stopped and glanced up at the sound of a discreet cough.

Devlin saw the aged retainer who had served his breakfast standing in the doorway. "Beg pardon, miss," he said to Estelle, "the Reverend Miles has arrived somewhat earlier than expected."

"Our dear, dear Reverend Miles," Estelle said to Devlin as she rose from the table, "is on his way to bear his cross in the Lake District and, since his parish there is reputed to be as poor as the dirt underfoot, Jane has kindly offered to send him on his way with some of the clothing left in the attic by Mr. Lyon. If you would excuse me, my lord."

"Of course," Devlin said, rising and bowing, "for though a man may speak with the tongues of angels, and have not charity, he is become as sounding brass, or a tinkling cymbal." My God, he thought, Estelle Winward's mode of speech was infectious.

"Thank you, my lord," Estelle said, "those are my sentiments to a fare-thee-well."

Left alone, Devlin lingered over his breakfast of eggs, toast, and chocolate, then strolled into the hall where he caught a glimpse of a black-garbed gentleman following Estelle Winward up the stairs. Ah, he told himself, that must be the Reverend Miles.

Making his way to the King's Room, he stood gazing at the cloak displayed on the tailor's dummy in the glass case. In the bright light of day the cloak seemed diminished, more time-worn and ordinary, but Devlin had eyes for nothing else. This must be the cloak he

sought, he assured himself, and soon, very soon, he
would force it to reveal its secret.

To him and him alone.

After carefully glancing around to make certain he
was unobserved, Devlin slid an oilskin packet from his
waistcoat pocket and drew forth a creased slip of paper. He stared at the jumble of letters and numbers,
puzzling over them as he had so often during these
last few months:

"D-O-N-E-C-6-1"

Meaningless letters, meaningless numbers. The
cloak would provide the key to unlocking their secret.
If not, there was no hope of success, none at all.

Open the case at once, he urged himself. Fortune
favors the daring, not the timid. Be bold, take the cloak
now. He reached out and was lifting the latch when
he heard the voice of Estelle Winward somewhere behind him. Be patient, he counseled himself as he relatched the case door, all in good time. Tonight, while
Lyon Hall slept, he would decipher the secret of the
cloak without running the risk of discovery.

After reluctantly leaving the King's Room, Devlin
strode from the house to the stable where Horatio, a
large black and white dog of indeterminate ancestry,
raced to greet him, yelping with delight. Leaning
down, Devlin smiled as he patted the dog's flank.

Unable to find a groom to assist him, Devlin sad-
dled one of his landau team, a chestnut gelding he
favored, mounted and rode toward the front of the
house with Horatio bounding along at his side. He
slowed, nodding as he rode by the Reverend Miles,

and the young man of the cloth, who was loading bundles into the back of his rig, swept off his hat and bowed in reply.

A moment later Devlin looked over his shoulder and discovered Horatio lagging far behind. He called to the dog only to be ignored as Horatio, quick off the mark, raced toward the house. Devlin caught a glimpse of a black cat in the drawing room window and then the cat was gone, leaving Horatio barking futilely up at the empty window. As though finally realizing how fruitless his pursuit had been, the dog turned and trotted back to his master.

Devlin rode on along the tree-bordered avenue, passing between the two weathered lions guarding the entrance to the Hall and, at the junction with the Midhurst Road, reined in beside his crippled landau. Cunningham, who had used planks to prop the carriage upright, was rolling the errant wheel toward its rightful place.

If anyone had been listening at that moment—no one, in fact was—he might very well have expected Lord Devlin to ask Cunningham when he expected to complete the repairs to the carriage. If so, he would have been surprised beyond measure to hear Cunningham ask, "How long, milord, would you be wanting this mounting of the wheel to take?"

"I would imagine the task will consume the better part, if not all, of the day," Devlin told him, "forcing me to request leave to spend another night at the Hall."

Cunningham nodded. "Very good, milord," he said with a knowing smirk.

"I fully intend to depart early tomorrow morning," Lord Devlin went on, "but, in case I must alter my plans, you and the carriage must be at the gate by midnight, prepared to leave at a moment's notice."

"We're away whenever you give the word, milord."

"Capital."

After giving Cunningham a nod of approval, Devlin rode on with Horatio first running ahead, then lagging behind. Devlin followed the Midhurst Road for a short distance before veering off to the right across a stream and into a field. He smiled, delighting in the glories of the October morning. A chill was in the air but, as he urged his gelding up a low hill, his face was warmed by the sun shining from the rain-washed sky. At the crest of the hill, he stopped to look out across the stubbled fields, the autumn-hued trees, the shrubs of the hedgerows and, in the far distance, the undulating South Downs.

Below him, perhaps a half mile from his vantage point, a lone rider galloped toward a dauntingly high rail fence. The horse leaped high, horse and rider seemed suspended in mid-air for a long breathtaking moment, and then came gracefully to earth, racing on without breaking stride.

"Well done, sir," Devlin murmured, "well done indeed."

Almost at once he realized his error. No, impossible, his eyes must be deceiving him. But impossible or not, he realized it was true—the rider astride the jet-black horse was not a he at all but a she, and not just any she but none other than Miss Jane Sterling of Lyon Hall. The fact that she rode astride had deceived him.

What else could you expect from an American? he asked himself as he shook his head in disapproval. Was she as unconventional in other ways as well? The daring Lady Caroline Lamb, or so they said, rode astride and *her* non-equestrian exploits were only too well known in the *ton*.

About to ride down the hill to join her, all at once Devlin held when he saw that Jane had reined to a halt. When he looked beyond her, Devlin saw another rider—and this, he was certain, was a man and not a woman—leave the cover of a copse and approach her. After he stopped her, the newcomer held out his hand, took Jane's, leaned over and raised it to his lips.

Devlin felt a sharp flush of anger. The stranger was guilty of trespass, he told himself. Almost at once he frowned, recognizing how unreasonable he was being and at the same time wondering why he was so perturbed. Had he taken complete leave of his senses? Why should he be vexed to discover Miss Sterling keeping a rendezvous with a stranger? Or was this a rendezvous he was observing? He could be mistaken, perhaps this was merely a chance meeting of two neighboring landowners. In his not inconsiderable experience, however, meetings between unaccompanied ladies and gentlemen were seldom completely unplanned.

But no, his suspicions must be unfounded. If this was a rendezvous, a tryst, surely Jane and the stranger would have chosen a more secluded spot. And certainly they would dismount. Although they appeared to be absorbed in their conversation and although Jane leaned forward with apparent eagerness while the stranger gestured with his riding crop, both remained mounted. Devlin's heart lifted.

Wait. There was something about that horseman that struck a chord. A tall man, this interloper—or so Devlin thought of him—wore a dark blue riding coat, breeches of a lighter blue and black top boots. His hat was festooned with what Devlin considered a ridiculous blue plume. By God, Devlin thought with rising alarm, he must be a Frenchman. Could it be possible both he and this stranger had come to Sussex for the same reason?

Devlin idly rubbed his right thigh where a small scar marked the spot a French bullet had found its mark during the Battle of Vittoria. Damn Napoleon, damn the French. Suddenly his breath caught as he recalled Estelle Winward telling him that Jane Sterling had French blood. Could he be witnessing not a romantic assignation, not a casual encounter, but something far more sinister, the meeting of two plotters in league against him? It was just like the French to use an innocent-appearing woman as either an agent or a pawn in one of their cunning conspiracies.

"By God," he muttered to Horatio, "we must be on our guard."

Swinging his horse around, Devlin started back toward the Hall with his unfailingly faithful dog trotting after him. Though in his heart of hearts he believed Jane Sterling to be guiltless, he was in no position to take risks now that he had his quarry in sight. He would confront her this evening at dinner and attempt to judge whether her conscience was clear.

After learning he was more than welcome to stay a second night as Miss Sterling's guest at Lyon Hall, Devlin spent much of the long afternoon walking from his bed chamber to the stairs, counting the number of his steps, descending to the lower hall, walking through the drawing room to the King's Room, returning by the same route to his chamber and then repeating the procedure again and again until at last he was satisfied.

At seven he joined Jane and Estelle in the drawing room for a glass of sherry.

"How very lovely you look," he impulsively murmured to Jane.

You *have* taken leave of your senses, my dear fellow, Devlin chided himself. Lovely? In that impossible get-up? Her high-necked, long-sleeved gown all but swept the floor and it was forest green velvet rather than the sheer and delicate white or palely tinted fabric favored by the chic young ladies of the *ton*. Though it did happen to be high-waisted in the current fashion, it was just not the thing, not the thing at all.

Nor, he noted with a twinge of disappointment, did it give him so much as a glimpse of the swell of her bosom or the turn of her ankle. Besides, the gown was rather plain, its only decoration two bands of black braid, one at the waist and another at the hem. But, he acknowledged, the gown's very simplicity did serve to accentuate the beauty of her face and the curled perfection of her vivid hair.

Why do you defend her, Devlin? he demanded. If she appeared in town in that gown she would be immediately labeled a provincial. He had no doubt the colonies—although he was aware the States were not a colony, he firmly believed they should be—failed to keep pace with the latest fashions, but now that she was in England surely Miss Sterling must have noticed her clothes were sadly out-of-date. In London, her gown would be greeted with raised eyebrows and knowing smiles concealed behind fluttering fans.

Still, he reflected, it was impossible to deny that the gown became her, besides being practical in this chill and cavernous mausoleum of a house.

Estelle, he noticed absently as he escorted the two ladies to the dinner table, wore a grey gown in the mode of the nineties.

After an exchange of pleasantries, Devlin decided the time of testing had arrived. He cleared his throat. "While riding this morning," he said with as innocent atone as he could muster, "I chanced upon another horseman, a tall chap garbed in blue with a feather in his hat."

"That must have been M. LaSalle," Jane said, "of Montcalm House."

Ah, Devlin thought, he was right, the stranger *was* French. But Devlin had not been able to detect the slightest trace of guilt either in her voice or expression, although he noted she had said nothing about meeting LaSalle during her morning ride.

"Although I have yet to set eyes on him," Estelle said, "M. Claude LaSalle is reputed to be exceedingly charming and handsome. For a Frenchman, that is."

"M. LaSalle is newly arrived in Sussex," Jane told him, "an even later arrival than myself. Only after Napoleon fled into exile on Elba was he free to leave France to make his home in England."

"This sceptered isle," Estelle said, closing her eyes, "this earth of majesty, this other Eden, this fortress built by nature, this precious stone set in the silver sea, this realm, this England." She opened her eyes to glance at Devlin. "William Shakespeare," she explained.

Devlin nodded impatiently, refusing to be distracted by the vagaries of Estelle Winward. "Being a Frenchman," he said to Jane, "I suppose your M. LaSalle showed little or no interest in the King's Cloak."

"He only learned of the cloak today," Jane told him, "when I chanced to meet him while taking my morning ride. I happened to mention your unexpected arrival, Lord Devlin, and your fascination with the King's Cloak. M. LaSalle inquired about the history of the cloak, very much as you did last night."

Was Jane telling the truth? Devlin wondered. Her manner seemed candid and sincere but it was possible she and LaSalle were playing a deep game. Whatever the truth of the matter, he was fortunate to have arrived at Lyon Hall when he had. Another few days and he might have been too late.

If Jane was truly the innocent she appeared, he had nothing whatsoever to fear. On the other hand, if this American woman and this Frenchman were secret partners, he would outthink, outwit, and outmaneuver both of them. Smiling confidently, Devlin changed the subject.

After dinner, he pleaded fatigue and excused himself. As he was leaving the dining room, he was unable to resist pausing for a last glimpse of Jane since this, without a doubt, would be the last time he would ever see her. She was looking at him, smiling at him, her green eyes—they were definitely green and not hazel—glowing in the candlelight, her marvelous hair haloing her exquisite face.

With a hidden sigh of regret, Devlin forced himself to turn and make his way up the stairs to his bed chamber. He could not allow himself to be distracted. Everything was in readiness, he had made all of his preparations with care. The waiting was almost over, the key to the prize that had eluded searchers for a hundred and fifty years would soon be his.

Tonight, as soon as the hall was dark and quiet, as soon as there was no danger of discovery—the King's Cloak!

Three

Lord Devlin settled himself in the armchair beside the window in his bed chamber and opened Gibbon's *Decline and Fall*. He had been reading the history of the Roman Empire during his spare moments for the last nine months, more than a few times falling asleep with the heavy volume beside him on his bed.

He enjoyed reading slowly, often pausing to underline passages that caught his fancy, occasionally closing the book to ponder what he read of that long-ago time when Rome ruled England and London was known as Londinium. In many ways, he thought, modern England resembled ancient Rome, for he considered his native land a great civilization besieged by barbarians from the east, not the Huns, Vandals, and the Goths but the French. He was troubled by the fact that, as the fall of its empire neared, the Roman rulers had entertained the multitudes with circuses while in recent years the Prince Regent had hosted extravagant parties at Carlton House and lavish displays of fireworks in the parks.

Tonight he had difficulty concentrating, finding himself rereading passages time after time. Closing his eyes, he imagined himself a Roman in a conquered land. "Bring in the prisoner," he ordered. A centurion led the woman into the room, her red hair disheveled, her green eyes flashing defiance, her warrior's garb torn. He smiled in triumph; she was his slave to do with as he chose.

Devlin shook himself from his reverie. Why, he wondered, did his thoughts return to Jane Sterling again and again?

Enough! He glanced impatiently at the pocket watch he had placed on the table beside his chair. How slowly the minutes ticked away, five, ten, fifteen, how interminable the passage of the hours, ten o'clock, eleven, twelve.

At a few minutes past twelve, he could abide the wait no longer. Standing, he looked down from the window at a lawn silvered by light from the moon high overhead, at the black hulk of the stable and the equally dark forest beyond. A feeble light shone from one of the Hall's kitchen windows, probably a candle left burning through the night.

Leaving his own candle burning, he crossed the room and eased open the door. The hallway was dark, the house quiet. He waited a minute, two minutes, alert, ready to retreat at any sign of life, atingle with anticipation. When he saw and heard nothing, he slipped into the hall and closed the door, leaving himself in darkness.

He walked slowly but confidently along the carpeted hall. Ten paces. He reached in front of him. Nothing. Another half-pace and he nodded with satisfaction when his hand touched the banister. He counted the steps as he descended, counted twenty-one in all. The lower hall was dark, the drawing room dimly lit by the glow of moonlight. He crossed to the archway to the King's Room, his heart pounding as he neared his goal.

A sound, a distant creaking, caused him to hold, his every sense alert, but the sound did not come again. The creaking, no doubt, he assured himself, was merely the old house settling as old houses were wont to do.

Light reflected palely from the glass of the display case; inside, the cloak was a dark shadow. Devlin unlatched the door of the case and slid the cloak from the tailor's dummy, relatched the door and stood holding the cloak in one hand while he caressed the smooth velvet with the other. The prize was his. Or soon would be.

This was much too soon to exult, he reminded himself. Long ago he had learned the danger of carelessness bred from over-confidence. There was always the slender possibility that this was not the cloak he had sought these many months. Merriweather's journal of his flight from London to France, a journal discovered only last spring in Paris, had, after all, recorded events occurring one hundred and sixty-seven years ago. Many things could and did alter in more than a century and a half.

Devlin carefully draped the cloak over his arm before retracing his steps through the drawing room and into the hall. He stopped at the foot of the stairs, sensing a change, an subtle alteration of the atmosphere warning of danger. Was it his imagination or did he feel a draft from a recently opened door or window? Hear a slight movement in the upper hall?

A small dark form hurtled down the stairway, startling him as it rushed past in the direction of the kitchen. His heart leapt. What the devil was it? He heard a hissing and sighed with relief when he realized he had been confronted by nothing more deadly than that damned black cat. What was his name? Chatter?

Relieved, Devlin started up the stairs. Twenty-one steps in all, he reminded himself. On the count of eighteen he paused, frowning. Why had the cat been wandering about the house at this hour of the night? Of course he knew little of the habits of felines since he much preferred the company of dogs. For some unfathomable reason, most women of his acquaintance favored cats over dogs even though they had no sense of loyalty; a cat, like a bit of muslin, bestowed her favors on the highest bidder.

Deciding that this particular cat must be a nocturnal animal accustomed to roaming the house by night and sleeping during the day, he firmly put the beast from his mind and ascended the final three steps.

The upper hall was quiet and within moments Devlin was inside his bed chamber with the door firmly closed behind him. Capital. He crossed the room and spread the cloak on the bed, probing the fabric with his fingers much as he had done the night before. Again, he discovered nothing. Turning the cloak over, he took his knife from the table beside the bed and carefully cut a foot-long slit along the edge of the satin lining. He reached inside the lining, his hand exploring every recess again and again, each time with increasing desperation.

"Hellfire and damnation," he muttered. He had found nothing.

Standing beside the bed with his hands on his hips, Devlin stared down at the blue cloak. For the first time he noticed a small label sewn on the lining near the bottom hem: "Kravitz Clothiers, 34 St. James Street." No, impossible, absolutely impossible. But the label was there and no amount of wishing would cause it to disappear.

He heard the door open behind him. He whirled around. Jane Sterling, wearing a grey afternoon dress, stood in the doorway, her green eyes blazing as she looked from him to the cloak and back again.

"Why have you taken the cloak?" she demanded.

Devlin shook his head. Snatching the cloak from the bed, he thrust it toward her. "This is not the King's Cloak," he rasped. "This is a fraud, a sham."

"Not the King's Cloak?" she echoed.

"Do you see this label?" Grasping the hem of the cloak, he held the label in front of her. "Kravitz Clothiers, St. James Street," he read, "a reliable establishment, to be sure, but they happen to date only from my father's day, not from the middle of the seventeenth century. You, me, everyone has been bamboozled. This garment is no more the King's Cloak than—than—"

"Than you, Lord Devlin? Are you an honorable man who would never think of taking something not his?"

He let the cloak fall to the carpet. "What—did—

you—say?" he asked, emphasizing each word, unable to believe he had heard correctly.

"You know full well what I said." Anger lent a cutting edge to her voice. "You, a benighted traveler who sought refuge in my house, saw fit to repay my hospitality by waiting until the dead of night when you thought we were all asleep and then proceeded to steal my cloak. And before you ask me to repeat myself, my exact words were, 'you proceeded to steal my cloak.' "

"Not *your* cloak, Miss Sterling," he said stiffly, "this is the King's Cloak. Or so I thought."

"Only a moment ago you claimed this was *not* the King's Cloak. Are you confused, my lord, or did I mishear you?"

"No, you heard aright, this cloak happens to be an impostor." He felt much like a fish must feel when, having become impaled on the hook, darts this way and that in an attempt to escape. "But the fact remains," he went on, "I truly believed it was the King's Cloak. And I did not steal the cloak, I merely borrowed it."

She smiled coldly, her high dudgeon replaced by an icy chill.

Despite his discomfiture at being taken unawares, he delighted in looking at her. Anger brought a flush to her cheeks and a glint to her green eyes, hinting at a passion only imperfectly concealed. She had dared to confront him, to question him, she seemed to take pleasure in plaguing him in every possible way; he had always delighted in facing and overcoming a challenge. He believed himself to be at his best when placed in a tight corner.

"Do you expect me to believe," she asked, "that you waited until almost one in the morning to borrow the cloak you believed to be the King's Cloak but which you now claim is not the King's Cloak?"

"Yes, and I also expect you to believe I borrowed the cloak not for any gain for myself but for your sake, Miss Sterling."

She slowly shook her head. "I strongly suspect that you, sir," she said, "are a fabulist, a dissembler. In America we have an even simpler and more telling word. Liar."

"Since you are obviously befuddled, my dear Miss Sterling, I choose to ignore all of your inaccurate and ill-chosen words, words you will regret when you know the truth of the matter."

"And what, pray tell, is the truth, Lord Devlin?"

"I borrowed the cloak for the purpose of determining its authenticity. When, last night, you described the dire financial condition of Lyon Hall, my heart went out to you since I found you to be a captivating young woman in the most distressing circumstances, and I decided, if the chance ever arose, to do all in my power to assist you. When a short while later I saw the cloak, I was struck by the possibility that your salvation might very well be at hand. The King's Cloak might be more valuable than you imagine."

She eyed him with suspicion but her anger seemed to have ebbed. "Truly valuable?" she asked with a touch of hope in her voice.

"Not as wearing apparel, certainly, but for its historical significance. Imagine, a cloak worn by kings!"

She frowned as if something troubled her. "Is that why you slit the lining?" she wanted to know. "To determine whether it was authentic?"

"The lining?" He glanced guiltily at the knife still laying on his bed. "Ah, yes, of course, the lining." He paused as he searched for a plausible answer. When he thought of one, his words came in a rush. "It happens to be a well-known fact. The age of velvet. The underside. The only certain method."

"I fail to follow you."

He smiled in what he hoped was a knowing way. "One of the best known methods of determining the age of velvet is to examine the underside of the fabric, the side not exposed to the elements. And that was what I was about to do when I noticed the Kravitz label and knew the cloak was of recent origin."

She sighed with exasperation. "There was no reason for you to skulk about in the dead of night to look at the reverse side of the velvet. If you had simply told me the cloak might be valuable, I would have gladly let you examine it at your leisure."

"You, Miss Sterling, must learn to be more trusting of your fellow man. You perceive evil intentions where there are none. Let me assure you, I was acting in your best interests. I had no desire to raise your hopes only to have them dashed if the cloak proved to be a sham or, if valuable, it failed to fetch a suitable price. So I did all in my power to discover if the cloak might have value *before* I confided in you."

"Now I understand, my lord. Everything you did

was for me. To protect my tender feelings, to provide me with funds."

Devlin nodded eagerly. "Just so, for you and no other. You surely realize how taken I am with you. At my first glimpse of you last night, I was struck by your amiability; nay, I found you more than amiable, I thought you absolutely enchanting." He may have shaded the truth a bit when she first found him in possession of the cloak, Devlin admitted to himself, but in this he was quite sincere.

Jane, he noted with satisfaction, was unable to hide her pleasure at his words.

"The cloak might be worth a considerable sum?" she asked.

"If it were authentic I believe there are those who would value it most highly since there are many admirers of the handsome and impetuous Charles I. But this, alas"—he nodded at the cloak on the floor—"is not Charles's cloak nor any king's cloak. Perhaps there never was such a cloak at Lyon Hall."

"Indeed there was such a cloak here," she told him, "and there still is."

Confused, he stared at her. "The label clearly dates the cloak—" he began.

"You happen to be quite correct, Lord Devlin, the cloak you spirited away is no older than yourself. I deemed it the height of foolishness to leave the real cloak on display in an unlocked cabinet and so I found a similar-appearing one and made the substitution."

"And the real cloak?" he asked, unable to hide his eagerness.

"Is quite safe in one of our attic storerooms."

Devlin drew in his breath and gave a long sigh of relief. "Splendid!" he cried. "You must take me to the authentic cloak at once." He needed to act with dispatch, he reminded himself, to keep the Frenchman—Claude LaSalle—from stealing a march on him.

Jane shook her head. "Consider the hour, milord. The cloak has waited for more than a hundred and fifty years, it can surely wait another few hours. The morning will be time enough."

Devlin started to protest but immediately checked himself. No matter how much he chafed at any delay, he must not overplay his hand, must not arouse her suspicions by appearing over-eager.

"As you wish," he conceded, forcing a smile and bowing, "we shall wait until morning."

"Capital." He wondered whether she was mocking him but her expression gave him no clue.

When Jane returned to her chamber she found Chatter curled on the foot of her bed. "Ah, Chatter," she told him, "you almost gave me away tonight."

The cat leaped down and curled around her ankles as though seeking to make amends. "But I forgive you," she said, picking up the cat and stroking his soft fur as she cradled him in her arms. "If only I could discover," she said, "the real reason Lord Devlin wants the cloak."

As she prepared for bed, she asked Chatter, "Do you find him attractive? No? But then, you are prejudiced since you dislike his dog. Horatio? Is that his name?"

Chatter showed no interest in either Lord Devlin or his dog.

"Men must be allowed their dogs, I suppose," Jane said. "I admit I do find him attractive, Devlin, that is, though impossibly proud. Not proud exactly, arrogant, as though he and his kind were God's gift to mankind. I do believe our good Lord Devlin needs taking down a peg or two. Perhaps we can see to that, what do you say, Chatter? But first we must discover why he wants the King's Cloak."

Still puzzling over Devlin's motives, Jane fell asleep almost as soon as her head touched her pillow and, when she awoke early the next morning, she was no closer to a solution to the mystery. Not for an instant did she believe Devlin had taken the cloak to help her save Lyon Hall from its creditors. And his explanation for slitting the lining of the cloak had been concocted from whole cloth. Tell the age of velvet from its underside, indeed! Evidently he thought something had been hidden in the lining but she had no notion what that something might be.

She rose early the next morning only to find Devlin waiting for her in the breakfast room. How eager he must be to find the cloak.

"I trust you slept well," she said with a smile.

"I did not." The shadows under his eyes gave evidence he spoke the truth.

"A guilty conscience is often a hindrance to a restful night," she said.

He looked at her in a speaking way but said nothing. Why, she wondered, did she take so much pleasure in goading him? She enjoyed his every scowl, took delight each time his eyes narrowed in annoyance. She had good reason, she told herself. He had deceived her, had given crooked answers when she accused him of deceit, he had taken advantage of her hospitality, he would do whatever he considered necessary to spirit the King's Cloak away from her.

She vowed not to let him.

Jane ate slowly, watching Devlin from the corner of her eye and taking satisfaction when she saw his increasing unease. Though he was clearly on tenterhooks, eager to abandon his meal at her slightest suggestion, he did his best to show a lack of concern.

Finishing her chocolate, Jane said, with all the innocence she could muster, "This is another fine October day, a grand morning for a ride. Would you care to accompany me, my lord?"

He glared at her in exasperation. "No," he thundered, "I will not!" He drew in a sharp breath. "We shall find the King's Cloak and we shall do it now."

"We shall?" she asked calmly.

"Yes," he said, putting both hands on the table, "for your sake, Miss Sterling."

She smiled amiably. "Your graciousness is only matched by your generosity in offering to help me find the wherewithall to keep Lyon Hall," she told him. Before he could reply, she said, "By all means, my lord, let me show you where I put the cloak for safekeeping."

"Splendid." Devlin rose and, with a flourish, drew back her chair.

Jane led the way into the hall, opening the door of a closet beneath the grand staircase. "We keep some of our keys here," she told him, removing a long metal key from a hook on the far wall.

He raised his eyebrows. "Hardly a prudent procedure."

"We have very little reason to lock and bolt our doors in Sussex. Since I arrived here last spring, there have been a few reports of poaching in the neighborhood but, to the best of my knowledge, no other thefts." She paused before adding, "Until last night."

Devlin's face reddened and he seemed on the verge of making a sharp retort but to her surprise he merely grimaced and remained silent. I really must stop goading him, Jane told herself, as she preceded him up the two flights of stairs to the second floor where she unlocked and opened a door revealing a steep stairway.

"This will take us to the storeroom in the west attic," she told him.

The stairs led directly into a cavernous, cluttered room under the wing's sloping roof. Light came from windows at each end; a massive brick chimney rose through the center.

She started to cross the storeroom.

"Wait," Devlin told her. Puzzled, she turned to him, saw him standing with his back to the window, his face in the shadow, staring at her. She started to ask him what he wanted but before she could speak he stepped toward her and something in his intense gaze made her breath catch. Her pulses raced.

He reached out and gently touched the side of her

face. She stood transfixed, expectant yet wary, aquiver yet fearful, wanting to believe in his gesture of affection while at the same time knowing it would be folly to trust him. His fingers slowly caressed her face, tracing the line of her chin; he leaned to her until he was but a breath away. Time stopped. He came closer still until his lips brushed against hers in a brief, tender kiss.

For an instant, only an instant, she closed her eyes as she was suffused by a tingling glow akin to the warmth of the sun on a summer meadow. She opened her eyes as first doubt and then anger surged through her. Devlin meant to beguile her, to use what he probably regarded as his devastating charm to weaken her resolve. His kiss was not affection, not a promise, it represented nothing more than a deceitful stratagem.

She drew back her arm, her fury as violent as a sudden storm sweeping across the countryside with lightning flashing and thunder rolling. He stepped away from her, a startled look on his face, backing against the railing at the head of the stairs. He held out his hand in a conciliatory gesture while at the same time shaking his head as though to assure her he meant no harm.

"It was an irresistible impulse," he said, his voice seemingly sincere. "When I look at you, Jane—Miss Sterling—when I breathe in that exquisite, intoxicating scent, I lose all sense of judgment, I act rashly. I refuse to beg your pardon, however, for I must admit I feel no remorse for what I did."

Although she believed not a word of what he said—

no matter how much she might want to believe each and every one of them—she lowered her hand. Though Lord Devlin might be incapable of acting the gentleman, she could still behave like a lady.

Without a word, Jane turned from him and walked across the attic, threading her way between brass-bound trunks and boxes containing the detritus of many years, stopping in front of an oak wardrobe. Hearing Devlin's footsteps behind her, she imagined his anticipation, his eagerness to find the real King's Cloak.

She pulled open one of the double doors of the wardrobe, peered inside and gasped. After opening the other door, she shook her head.

"What is it?" Devlin demanded. "Is something wrong?"

"The cloak was here yesterday," she said, gesturing futilely at the empty wardrobe, "but now it's gone."

Four

Devlin knelt in front of the wardrobe and reached inside, groping into each of its dark corners in search of the cloak. "Empty," he said. "The King's Cloak *is* gone." He glanced up at Jane. "Are you certain this is where you put it?" he asked.

"Quite certain," she told him. "I carried the cloak here to the west wing attic early yesterday morning after I noticed your extraordinary interest in it the night before. I feared you might do what in fact you did do."

Devlin stood, brushing off the knees of his breeches. "Then someone has made off with the King's Cloak either by chance or by design." He gave her a sharp look. "Was that Frenchman, M. LaSalle, a visitor at Lyon Hall yesterday?"

Jane shook her head, puzzled by his question. "No, not to my knowledge. Why do you ask? Why should M. LaSalle be interested in the cloak? My cloak." Mine more than any long-dead king's, she reminded herself.

"He *is* French and we English have been at war

with the French for many years. He might very well consider the cloak akin to a trophy of war."

What an odd notion, Jane thought, once again suspecting Devlin was skirting the truth to conceal the reason for his interest in the cloak. "Even if M. LaSalle coveted the cloak," she told him, "he would have had no notion where it might be. Nor even a good idea of what it looked like since he has never been inside Lyon Hall."

"Be that as it may, cloaks are not in the habit of disappearing into thin air. There must be an explanation."

"And probably a very simple one."

They were both silent for a time as they pondered the mystery and then they both spoke at once: "The Reverend Miles."

"Yesterday morning," Devlin said, "I saw Miss Winward leading him upstairs."

"Unfortunately, Aunt Estelle is inclined to be somewhat scatterbrained. She could well have become confused and brought him to the wrong storeroom, come here to the west wing rather than the east."

"We must find out," Devlin said, starting across the floor toward the top of the stairs only to stop after a few steps to wait for her to accompany him.

How anxious Lord Devlin is, Jane thought, as she walked to the stairs with him. Why does the cloak mean so much to him? She almost felt sorry for Devlin as he encountered one disappointment after another. He did not, though, deserve one iota of her sympathy for he had certainly not been candid with her.

They found Estelle sitting in front of the fire in the drawing room, her head bent over her embroidery. "St. Paul's Cathedral," she told them, displaying the half-finished result of her handiwork. "When I think of London, which I admit I often do, I always think of Christopher Wren and St. Paul's."

Devlin, obviously impatient, started to speak but Jane silenced him with a cautionary shake of her head. She would not allow him to alarm Estelle who, for all her confused rambling, had proved to be both loyal and caring, a treasure.

After sitting on the settee and motioning Devlin to a place beside her, Jane said, "When we were in the west wing of the attic, Aunt Estelle, we discovered that the wardrobe was empty. By any chance did the Reverend Miles—?"

"Oh, yes," Estelle said, smiling, "the dear man took every last scrap of clothing and left here pleased as punch. 'Blessed are the pure in heart such as yourself and Miss Sterling,' he said to me as he bade me goodbye, 'for they shall see God.' "

Devlin leaned forward. "And you gave him the clothing for his new parishioners in the Lake District from the wardrobe in the *west* wing of the attic?" he wanted to know.

Estelle lowered her head and closed her eyes in thought. "The west wing rather than the east wing?" she asked.

"Precisely," Devlin said.

Estelle looked up, opened her eyes and smiled. "The west wing to be sure, my lord. I tell the wings apart, you see, by the keys. The key to the west wing is long and silver and the key to the east wing is short and black and so instead of attempting to recall whether I want the east or the west—the four points of the compass are so confusing, after all—I ask myself, 'Which key shall I use?' and if what I want is in the west wing I say to myself, 'Use the silver key,' and if in the east wing I say, 'Use the black key.' " The older woman frowned. "Or is it the other way around?"

Jane glanced at Devlin, raising her eyebrows slightly. Devlin sighed.

"Whatever is the matter?" Estelle looked from Jane to Devlin and suddenly gasped. "Can it be the Reverend Miles took the wrong clothes?"

"We believe," Devlin told her, "that he left Lyon Hall not only with the wrong clothes but with the King's Cloak as well."

"Oh dear, oh dear." Estelle's face crumpled; she appeared close to tears. "I do become addled at times," she admitted.

Jane covered the other woman's hand with her own. "I shall write to the Reverend Miles this very morning," she promised, "and request him to return the cloak at his earliest convenience."

"Oh dear, oh dear, you may be too late. As kindhearted as he is, the dear man may well have already given it away by the time he receives your letter."

"He may indeed, unless I prevent him," Lord Devlin said, rising and striding to the door.

Jane followed him into the hall. "Wait," she said, "what do you intend to do?"

He turned to her. "As soon as Cunningham has the landau ready, and I expect he does by now, I plan to overtake Mr. Miles, inform him of the error, and return the cloak to Lyon Hall."

She nodded. "I shall go with you."

Devlin's face darkened. "You? Drive north to the Lake District with me? Decidedly not. An altogether preposterous notion."

Unflinching, she met his angry gaze. Devlin looked away first and started to walk toward the rear of the house. She was about to follow him when he turned and strode past her into the drawing room.

From the doorway Jane watched him cross the room to where Estelle, her eyes misting, sat with her embroidery hoop abandoned on her lap. He knelt in front of the older woman. "You have no need to fret," Jane heard Devlin tell her. "I promise you the King's Cloak will be returned to Lyon Hall within the week."

Estelle murmured a question Jane was unable to hear.

"Without a doubt," Devlin assured her with a most engaging smile. "You have the personal guarantee of Lord Devlin." Rising, he gallantly took her hand and brought it to his lips.

"God bless you, my lord," Estelle said, smiling up at him.

When Devlin returned to the hall, he glanced at Jane before hurrying on without a word. How kind of him to return to comfort Estelle, she thought, only to have doubt slither into her mind. Could it be his assurances to the older woman arose not from a natural impulse but were merely Devlin's way of enlisting Estelle as his ally?

Jane was starting to follow him to, she supposed, the stable, determined to accompany him in pursuit of the Reverend Miles, when Hendricks approached proffering a letter on his tray. "The morning post, miss," he told her.

A glance at the letter's cover told her the message came from her solicitor in Haslemere.

"Begging your pardon, miss," Hendricks said with his usual deference, "I hesitate to interfere in family affairs but Joshua told me something I believe you should be made privy to."

What could the butler have learned from the stableboy? Jane wondered. "Pray tell me, Hendricks," she said.

"Joshua is up and about at the first cock crow," Hendricks said, "and yesterday morning, him being a curious sort, he walked to the gate for a look at his lordship's carriage. What he saw struck him as more than passing strange."

"And what did he see?"

"Joshua swears that the wheel never left that carriage either by accident or misadventure. Someone deliberately removed it."

"Lord Devlin's accident was a ruse?" Jane's voice showed her shock and surprise.

"So Joshua says and I believe him, Joshua being a truthful lad and one what knows his way around horses and carriages better than most. And I say that, miss, not just because of his being the orphaned son of my dear departed nephew."

"Thank you for telling me, Hendricks, and thank Joshua as well," she said. "And please ask Alice to pack my things for a week's journey."

"Very well, miss," Hendricks said, unable to completely conceal his surprise and curiosity.

After the butler left, Jane stared unseeing at the letter clutched in her hand, her thoughts on what Hendricks had told her. So Devlin had come to Lyon Hall not by any happenstance but as a result of his own clever hoax. He must have heard stories of the King's Cloak and laid plans to force himself upon her as an overnight guest. Accustomed to scheming and plotting himself, he naturally suspected M. LaSalle of similar deviousness. Was there no end to Devlin's villainy?

Becoming aware of the letter, she slit open the seal and scanned the tiny, precise script. "It is my unhappy duty to inform you that if, at the end of ninety days," Mr. Grundage concluded his melancholy account, "these obligations have not been satisfied in their entirety, Lyon Hall must, perforce, be placed under the jurisdiction of the court and henceforth sold to the highest bidder."

Jane sighed even though the news was not unexpected. Ninety days would be the end of January. She had so little time.

She wistfully recalled how hopeful she had been when Lord Devlin arrived at Lyon Hall two days before, thinking what she considered his chance coming augured well for her and for the estate. Now she realized he had not followed her blaze of candlelight but had deliberately sought out the Hall because of the King's Cloak.

The cloak could still, she reasoned with what she admitted was more hope than logic, be the means to save Lyon Hall. The cloak must be indeed valuable to induce Devlin to lie and steal since, despite the mounting evidence to the contrary, in her heart she suspected he considered himself to be an honorable man and perhaps was, at least under ordinary circumstances. Fortunately, the cloak did not belong to Devlin nor to a king dead these hundred and sixty years; the cloak belonged to her.

The cloak is mine and no one—no one—will take it from me! Jane vowed.

On her way to find Lord Devlin, she heard the thud of hoofbeats and, glancing from a side window, she drew in her breath when she saw the landau drive by. She had tarried too long, Devlin was on his way without her. Turning, she hastened to the front door.

She sighed with relief to find the landau waiting at the foot of the stone steps, the two horses pawing the gravel of the sweep, impatient to be away, and Cunningham ensconced in his place on the driver's seat, the reins in his hand. Devlin, though, was not in the carriage nor anywhere else within sight.

"Where is Lord Devlin?" she asked Cunningham.

"By the stable, miss," the coachman told her.

Walking rapidly around the side of the house she saw Devlin, his back to her, his arms folded over the top rail of a fence. Some distance beyond him, in a field on the other side of the little-used horse-walking ring, Horatio raced toward Joshua gripping a stick in his mouth.

She stopped, watching Devlin, Joshua, and the dog, struck by Devlin's ease of manner. Somehow he seemed to belong here at Lyon Hall. Perhaps she, the American, was the one who did not belong.

"Horatio!" Devlin called just as Joshua took the stick from the dog and drew back his arm to hurl it again.

The dog looked at Devlin, barked happily, glanced up at Joshua and the stick but then opted to run to his master. Devlin patted him, turned and, seeing Jane, started toward her. Joshua, the stick still held in his hand, stared after Devlin and the dog trotting at his side.

"I was returning to the Hall," Devlin told Jane after a suggestion of a bow, "to thank you for your hospitality before I departed for the north. I give you every assurance you shall have the cloak in your possession as soon as humanly possible."

"I expect I shall, Lord Devlin," she said with a polite smile, "since I have every intention of being with you when you overtake the Reverend Miles. Kindly inform Cunningham I shall be ready to accompany you within thirty minutes, an hour at the very most."

"Ah, my dear Miss Sterling, unfortunately that will be absolutely impossible," he said with an air of exaggerated courtesy.

Determined not to let what she took to be his condescension anger her, Jane remained calm while vowing to hold her ground, come what may.

"I depart directly," Devlin said, "and my journey will be a long and arduous one since Mr. Miles, that good man of the cloth, has more than a twenty-four hour start. I suppose you, Miss Sterling, could venture to travel north in your own conveyance but after a cursory inspection of that vehicle—it must be all of twenty years old—I would hesitate to recommend journeying beyond Midhurst."

"True enough, the Lyon Hall carriage is not to be trusted for long journeys. Therefore, seeing that your landau has experienced a miraculous recovery, I shall travel with you to find Mr. Miles and recover the cloak. You seem to believe the cloak belongs to you, Lord Devlin, but it happens to be mine. What will Mr. Miles think and what will he do when confronted with a stranger, yourself, demanding he surrender the cloak?"

Devlin shrugged as though the ownership of the cloak was of little importance. "You may rest assured that after I recompense Mr. Miles for any inconvenience he may have suffered, the good preacher will be able to afford fifty cloaks, nay, a hundred and fifty cloaks. So you see, Miss Sterling, your presence would do nought but impede me in my pursuit of the Reverend Miles."

"Impede you. Not likely since I happen to be perfectly capable of looking after myself as I did for years in Louisiana and have these last six months in Sussex."

"You have no notion of the abominable state of traveling here in England and, if we were forced to drive all the way to the Lake District, we would be on the road for at least four days, probably five. The roads are deplorable, the tolls are exorbitant, the innkeepers along the way are insolent, the hostlers are sulky, the chambermaids are pert and the waiters are impertinent; the meat they serve at the inns is tough, the wine is foul, the sheets are damp, the linen is dirty, the bugs are ever-present and the knives are never cleaned."

"Surely you exaggerate."

"Only slightly, if at all. Not only would you be deucedly uncomfortable and a hindrance to me, you would do irreparable damage to your reputation. In fact you would find it completely shattered. Perhaps in the wilds of western America virtuous unattached females gallivant about town and country with men, but in England they do not. They most emphatically do not. If you traveled with me, before the end of the journey your good name would be more tattered than the King's Cloak. Propriety demands you act with perfect prudence."

"I have little to fear on that score, my lord, since in England I have no reputation, either good or bad, to protect. Besides, you are, are you not, an honorable man?"

"Regrettably, no man is capable of being completely honorable where an attractive woman is concerned."

"I agree with your maxim but I accept the risk."

Devlin stepped toward her, his brown eyes glinting, a half-smile on his lips. "We would be together constantly, you and I," he murmured, "forced to be in close proximity by day and by night, alone together in the carriage and in the inns along the way. Only imagine, if you will, what a scandal the *ton* would make of that."

Only imagine. The words echoed in her mind as she closed her eyes. Imagine herself and Devlin, the two of them alone together.

Night, a full moon rising, Devlin coming to her from out of the shadows, his hand touching the side of her face, caressing her as her heart pounded, Devlin whispering endearments, Devlin taking her into his arms, his lips seeking and finding hers, his kiss tender at first but then insistent, her gasp of surprise, her arms reaching out to enfold him, to draw him closer, her lips surrendering to his demands. . . .

"Miss Sterling. Jane."

When she opened her eyes to see him staring down at her, she felt a vivid flush spread over her face. For a moment she stood looking at him, unable to speak.

"Are you all right?" he wanted to know, concern in his voice.

Words eluded her; she could only nod. Though she was *not* all right by any means. She felt all at sea, confused and feverish, as though she was on the verge of coming down with some strange malady. Could it be that she wanted to accompany him for reasons she failed to completely understand? No, the cloak was all-important, the cloak was her last hope of saving Lyon Hall.

"You do agree?" he asked. "That it would be impossible for you to accompany me?"

She drew in a deep breath, dispelling the last traces

of her imaginings, quelling her discomfiture. "I do not agree," she told him stubbornly, "not at all. I am totally uninterested in what the *ton* might make of our search for the King's Cloak."

Devlin raised his hands in exasperation. "I can see clearly that further arguing will do nothing to sway you. Therefore, whether with your agreement or without it, I shall leave at once. And I shall travel alone." He bowed. "I bid you *adieu,* Miss Sterling."

He walked past her to the waiting landau and, without waiting for Cunningham, opened the door, climbed inside and sat down. when he patted the seat at his side, Horatio leaped up to join him.

"Thank you again," he said to Jane as he raised his hat. "Have no fear, I shall return the cloak as soon as I possibly can. Goodbye," he called, "goodbye, Miss Sterling."

She glanced away from Devlin to hide her tears. There was nothing she could do to stop him from leaving, she had shot the last arrow from her quiver. But she should try to put as brave a face on her defeat as possible, she should wish him goodbye or, as he had said earlier, *adieu.*

Adieu. Wait, she did have another arrow in her quiver, once she should have thought of long before this. "Lord Devlin!" she cried, turning to him just as he was rapping on the inside of the carriage to signal Cunningham to be away.

"A moment," Devlin ordered, stopping Cunningham just as the coachman raised his whip. "Miss Sterling, do you have a final word for me?" he asked, looking down at her from the window.

"I expect I shall see you before you return to Lyon Hall," she told him, "since I have no intention of remaining here to wait. I shall pursue Mr. Miles myself and I fully expect to overtake him before you do."

"And how, pray tell, will you be able to accomplish such a remarkable feat?"

"While your landau may be fast and Mr. Cunningham may be a skilled reinsman, I do believe M. LaSalle's coach will prove even faster."

"M. LaSalle?" he echoed.

"M. Claude LaSalle, my neighbor. Time after time M. LaSalle has offered to place his coach and four at my disposal. I have not the slightest doubt he will do so again." While M. LaSalle had promised to assist her in any way possible, she suspected his offer might turn out to be mere politeness if put to the test. But there was no reason for Devlin to know that; she certainly had no reason to tell him.

Devlin glowered at her.

"Not only do I believe he will allow me the use of his coach," Jane went on, "I suspect he will be more than willing to accompany me while I overtake Mr. Miles and retrieve the King's Cloak."

Devlin muttered under his breath.

"I beg your pardon, my lord?"

"I said, 'The devil take him,' " Devlin told her. He shook his head and sighed a deep sigh. "My dear Miss Sterling," he said, "when will you be ready to join me on my journey north?"

Her heart leaped. "In thirty minutes, my lord," she promised.

"I shall wait here." Folding his arms, Devlin sat back against the leather seat.

"I have one request," she said. "While Horatio may be the best of traveling companions, he shall have to sit on the roof."

"The roof? Horatio?" Devlin started to protest only to frown and sigh again. "I have a much better notion." Climbing to the ground, he looked about him, saw Joshua watching them, and called to the boy.

When Joshua came running, Devlin gestured toward his dog. "Would you look after Horatio until I return?" he asked.

The boy nodded eagerly.

Devlin reached into his pocket, took out a coin and spun it toward Joshua. The boy plucked it from the air. "A sovereign for your trouble," Devlin said.

The boy stared open-mouthed at this unexpected largesse.

As though uncomfortable to have his kindness observed, Devlin glanced at Jane. "You have precisely twenty-five minutes to make ready, Miss Sterling," he warned her, "no more."

Hiding a smile, Jane hurried up the steps and into the Hall. She had won this skirmish with Lord Devlin but, she realized, the final battle for the King's Cloak was still to be fought.

Five

Cunningham's whip cracked and they started forward with Jane waving goodbye to Estelle from the open window of the carriage. She kept looking back, wondering if she had been too hasty, wondering when she would see Lyon Hall again, and then they drove into the woods and the Hall disappeared from her view. In a few minutes they rattled between the twin lions guarding the gate and onto the road to London.

When she glanced at Lord Devlin sitting with arms folded in the corner diagonally opposite hers, she found him regarding her warily. Though he had greeted her cordially enough when she entered the carriage on her return from the Hall, his gaze lingering appreciatively on the pale blue redingote she wore over her high-necked grey carriage dress, he had immediately fallen silent. To Jane, he seemed like a host suffering an unwelcome guest while praying for her early departure.

Sauce for the goose, she reminded herself, sauce for the gander. Only two days before *he* had been the one forcing himself on her at Lyon Hall. She wondered if she should tax him at once with her knowledge that his supposedly chance arrival had not been the result of happenstance at all but a carefully contrived hoax. No, she would wait for a more opportune moment.

As they were crossing the stone bridge over the stream that marked the northern boundary of Lyon Hall, Lord Devlin uncrossed his arms and, standing, reached onto the rack above his head. What was he about? she wondered. To her surprise, he took a bulky volume from the rack, resumed his seat and, without so much as a glance at her, began to read.

Jane resented being ignored. "I feel certain," she said, watching for his reaction from the corner of her eye, "that the Reverend Miles will be pausing at a village near Worcester on his journey to the Lake District."

Devlin snapped his book shut and gave her a sharp glance. "And why will he do that?"

She slowly smoothed her grey gloves before answering. "His older brother, Frederic," she told him, "is curate at Malvern and last week Mr. Miles told me he expected to pay him a visit on his way north."

"Ahh," Devlin said. "That alters my plans."

"*Our* plans."

"Now I shall change horses later this evening in town," he said as though not hearing her, "and then proceed north for a few more hours before stopping for the night. With good weather and passable roads, we should reach Malvern tomorrow afternoon and, if fortune is with us, recover the cloak with no further ado."

Devlin again opened his book only to look up at

her almost at once. "Do you have any other helpful information, Miss Sterling," he asked with the exaggerated courtesy that he seemed to adopt when annoyed or angry, "that you might wish to share with me? Something that might assist in this endeavor?"

"None that comes to mind," she told him.

He nodded and resumed reading but now he seemed less engrossed in the book since, when he noticed her staring at the book's cover as she tried to make out the title, he said, *"The Decline and Fall of the Roman Empire,* Miss Sterling."

"Thank you, Lord Devlin."

Placing his forefinger between the pages and closing the book, he said, "Since we two shall be rather intimately associated, one with the other, for the next few days, may I make a suggestion designed to simplify whatever conversation may become necessary?"

How very wordy he could be! Did all Englishmen employ six words where one would suffice? "Of course," she said, answering him as simply as she could.

"I propose that I address you as Jane rather than Miss Sterling while you may call me Charles instead of Lord Devlin. Do you find that agreeable?"

"I prefer to call you Devlin if I may," she said. "To me, Devlin seems a much more appropriate name for you than Charles."

"Appropriate? Have you by any chance been amusing yourself by re-arranging the letters of my name in an attempt to discern my true character?" Suddenly he smiled as though at a fond memory. "I admit I often

did the same when I was a boy," he told her. "Word
games never ceased to amuse me."

"That notion never occurred to me but allow me to
try." She paused as she jumbled the letters of Devlin's
name in her mind, then smiled. "I would hesitate before calling you vile, Devlin. Or before I thought of
you as evil."

"But perhaps I may appear to you as being something of a devil? Someone from the nether regions sent
to Sussex for the purpose of plaguing you?" His smile
told her he found pleasure in his notion.

"No, but you might be said to wear a veil to hide
your true intentions."

"Enough! I perceive that very little indicating what
I might be like will ever be derived from the spelling
of *my* name. Sterling, on the other hand, speaks for
itself, suggesting the pure, the genuine, the excellent,
the exceptional. Devlin and Sterling. Our names would
say we are quite different even though the two of us
have so much in common."

"Pray tell me what we have in common. Very little,
I would think."

"No, no, a great deal," he told her. "To be specific,
the E, L, I, and N of both our names." Devlin nodded
as he named each of the letters.

Nile, she thought. Line. Lien. None of which made
any sense. "And nothing else?" she asked.

"Precious little else, I fear." He frowned as though
belatedly recalling how unwelcome he found her presence in his carriage.

Devlin immediately re-opened his book and started

to read of ancient Rome despite being jolted again and again as the carriage jounced toward London. From time to time, she noted, he would close his eyes and, when he opened them, glance across at her with his lips slightly parted, the speculative look in his eyes causing her a vague unease.

She gave up attempting to engage him in conversation. Looking from the window, she saw they were driving through a forest and, when she smelled smoke, she wondered if the woods were ablaze but almost at once she saw axe-wielding woodsmen felling and trimming large trees and, moments later, a barren expanse where piles of brush burned between the stumps of once-mighty oaks.

After leaving the forest, they stopped to eat at a roadside inn. When, as they were leaving, she said in a low voice, "Not *all* their knives were dirty," he smiled and said, "I may have exaggerated, I admitted as much at the time. You must concede, though, that these roads are much as God left them after the flood."

As they once again drove northward, Jane became aware they were nearing London by the number of other travelers thronging the road—horsemen and footmen, carriages of every style and size and shape, wagons and open carts and covered carts, long, square and double coaches, chaises, gigs, buggies, curricles, and phaetons. The sound of their wheels on the loose gravel of the road reminded her of the rush of waves on an ocean beach.

All at once she felt a sense of emptiness, of loneliness. A stranger in a strange land, she had found a calm harbor at Lyon Hall. Why had she impulsively weighed anchor to set sail on a rough and foreign sea aboard a ship captained by a man she hardly knew?

"Look there," Devlin said.

Shaking herself from her reverie and looking in the direction of his nod, she saw a gentleman and lady riding side by side along a dirt road.

"Pray note," Devlin said, "how the young lady rides not astride but using a sidesaddle. Although I suppose you care not a whit what others may do."

"To my way of thinking," she said, "the use of a sidesaddle is a most impractical method of riding, being both slow and awkward."

"But, according to more than one eminent physician, most beneficial to one's physical well-being."

"If so, how strange that gentlemen insist on riding astride."

"As you well know, there are great differences between gentlemen and ladies." His face flushed. "If I offended you, Jane," he said, "I beg your pardon. You have a knack of leading me down verbal garden paths."

"Have you noticed how men habitually seek to blame women for their own shortcomings, for their failures?" she asked sweetly. *"That* is one of the great differences between them."

"Women are never content to conclude a conversation unless they have the last word. Men, on the other hand, are more obliging. That is still another difference."

When she sat silent, Devlin said, "How strangely

mute you are all of a sudden. Do you have nothing to say in reply?"

"Nothing whatsoever, not a solitary last word. Thus proving you in error once again."

When Devlin raised his eyebrows and then scowled in exasperation, she reached out, intending to touch his arm to show she was only funning him but quickly changed her mind and withdrew her hand. Men had a tendency to misunderstand what were meant as friendly gestures.

"I learned to ride astride in Louisiana," she told him. "When my father, a ship's captain, was away at sea, as he was more often than not, I lived with Danielle Pariot, a cousin of my mother's who kindly welcomed me to her husband's small and rather poor plantation north of New Orleans."

"Where sidesaddles were unheard of?" he asked after they were passed through a tollgate and drove from the gravel road onto the cobbles.

"I was raised with the three Pariot sons," she said, "and since Cousin Danielle was sickly I rode and hunted and fished with the boys, learning little of women's ways but a great deal of men's."

"What a strange upbringing, but perhaps common in America."

Jane shrugged. "I never thought it strange since I knew no other. At the time I believed the way I was raised to be perfectly natural though nothing like that of the young girls in New Orleans, of course." She regarded him with pursed lips. "Have you ever thought that the way you must have been raised might be considered by many to be quite out of the ordinary?"

"And so, I suppose, it was, spending most of my youth in London." He nodded to the window of the carriage. "Which is where we are," he told her.

They were crossing a long, high balustraded bridge—Westminster Bridge, Devlin told her—with its bays and hooped lampposts. Although it still lacked several hours until sunset, they drove through a murky twilight caused by the dark cloud of smoke hovering over the rooftops. Below them, she saw the lights of the city gleaming and shimmering from the dark waters of the Thames like diamonds displayed on black velvet. Boats of every description, from rowboats to skiffs to schooners to barkentines to wherries to barges, thronged the river.

"How beautiful," Jane murmured, "despite the soot fouling the air. I can actually taste the grit."

"London is the greatest city in the world," Devlin said as he looked eagerly from the window, "one of the oldest cities of Europe but one that is constantly renewing itself. It is a huge sprawling monster, a city of contrasts, a place of pagans and debauchees living in the shadow of the magnificent dome of St. Paul's, of filth and stench alongside grandeur. A city of the impossibly rich and the excruciatingly poor, of splendor and squalor, a hundred cities combined into one with an enchanting vista around every corner. Samuel Johnson said that if a man ever tired of London, he must be tired of life. I agree. I never have my fill of London."

She stared at him, surprised by his passion. This was not the first time today he had surprised her, Jane reminded herself, recalling his kindness to Estelle and to Joshua. Devlin, she decided, was not merely the arrogant aristocrat she had assumed him to be. The better she came to know Devlin, the more she liked him. On the other hand, she had best not forget his devious, dark side.

"Americans have always been partial to London," Devlin told her. "There are even those who claim that when good Americans die they go to London."

"And when bad Americans die?"

"Why, they are doomed to remain in America, of course."

She tried to punish him with a sharp glance but, amused by his sally, proceeded instead to reward him with a smile which, she noted, he accepted as no more than his due.

Frowning as though he had allowed himself to be unnecessarily distracted, Devlin peered from the window. They had, she saw, driven down from the bridge, but before she could ask where they were, Cunningham halted the landau in front of a massive stone building, sprang to the roadway and opened the carriage door.

"Whitehall," Devlin told her cryptically. "Pray excuse me, I shall only be a moment."

He was scowling when he returned to the carriage a few minutes later. As they rumbled away, he said, "All of London seems to be in Vienna."

Seeing the throngs crowding the streets, she said, "Surely not all."

"The Prince Regent has stayed in town," he told her, "but Castlereigh and most of the others have left to take part in the Congress of Vienna which, I was told, commences tomorrow, the first day of November. Now that Napoleon is in exile on Elba, the great powers of Europe expect to conclude a peace that will last a hundred years or more." He shook his head to show what he thought of that notion.

Never mind the Congress of Vienna and Napoleon, Jane was tempted to say, did your stopping here have any bearing on our search for the King's Cloak? Reluctantly, she decided to hold her tongue. If he wished to tell her he would, if not, no words of hers would induce him to change his mind.

They drove past royal parks and then elegant mansions along both sides of stately streets and clustered around magnificent squares. "This is Mayfair," Devlin told her. As they passed a terrace of houses, he nodded, saying, "My town house. My Aunt Charlotte, a great favorite of mine, lives only a short distance to the west. We have, however, no time to spare." As he spoke, they entered a mews, stopping at a stable.

After only a brief pause to change horses they drove on to the north and then turned to the west as the twilight deepened into a cloudy, moonless night. Sooner than she expected, they left London behind to once more drive between country fields. Jane was settling back in her seat when she noticed a bonfire burning on a hill to her right, then another fire far off to her left, and presently a third on the crest of still another hill.

"Are those fires signals of some sort?" she asked Devlin, recalling that victories in battle were often proclaimed by bonfires.

"No, this is a pagan celebration," he told her with a dismissive wave of his hand, "a relic from the past, from before even the Romans. The fires are set by superstitious country folk."

Their carriage crossed a stream, drove into a copse and came out onto open, level ground. "Look at that hilltop," Jane said, leaning forward for a better view. "Do I see aright? Are those men and women holding hands while dancing around a bonfire?"

"They are indeed. If we were nearer we could probably hear them shouting 'Fire! Fire! Burn the witches. Fire! Fire! Burn the witches.' "

"Witches in 1814? Do the English still really believe in witches?"

"I expect a large number of my countrymen and women do. If not believe in them, most would admit the possibility they exist. Tomorrow, you see, is All Hallow's Day and so this is All Hallow's Eve. Centuries ago the Celts or the Druids or some other ancient inhabitants of this island marked the arrival of winter on the first day of November and, because each new day began at sunset rather than midnight, their festival started at nightfall. Supposedly the fires ward off the witches and demons who are abroad tonight on their way to observe their unholy sabbath."

Jane shivered in spite of herself. She was not in the

least superstitious, or she told herself, but the notion of witches and demons discomfited her. She recalled all too well the whispers of zombies and of strange voodoo rites she had heard in New Orleans.

When they passed through a village, she saw men and women wearing grotesque masks and costumes walking arm and arm along the streets.

"Those are guisers," Devlin said, "going from house to house, singing and dancing to mark the beginning of winter and to ward off evil spirits. For some reason the spirits, or so they claim, always fly toward the west, never toward the east."

Following the sun? Jane asked herself, then shook her head. No, spirits of the night most certainly would follow the moon and not the sun. But, of course, this was all mere superstition.

As they drove on in the darkness of the night, Jane tried to sleep but, though she was lulled by the swaying of the carriage and the rhythmic clip-clop-clip-clop of the horses' hooves, sleep eluded her. She felt a strange unease, a sensation that something was terribly wrong, that danger lurked she knew not where. There was nothing to fear, she told herself, nothing at all. She had allowed herself to be influenced by the bonfires, the masks, and Devlin's talk of pagan celebrations.

When she did doze off she was awakened almost at once by the clatter of the carriage wheels on stones and the shouts of men. Opening her eyes, she looked from the window to discover they had entered the courtyard of a country inn.

"This is the Angel Inn at Hellingdon," Devlin told

her, "a hostelry warmly recommended to me some years ago by a friend."

Cunningham returned from the inn with welcome news. Despite the lateness of the hour, he reported, Lord Devlin would be able to share a room with another gentleman while Jane could sleep in the room of a chambermaid, Betsy by name, who had departed earlier that same day to visit her aunt in Oxford.

Leaving the horses to Cunningham and the ostler, Devlin escorted Jane to a benchlike table in the dining hall, a cavernous, smoky room redolent with the odors of stale food and tobacco. Four young gentlemen, gallants all and all obviously the worse for drink, peered at the two of them through the haze. When one of the four rose unsteadily to his feet and made a leg as he doffed his hat to Jane, she looked quickly away.

Devlin muttered something under his breath. Shaking his head, he said, "Best to ignore them."

Only when the meal was served did she realize how hungry she was, matching Devlin forkful by forkful in laying waste to the mutton, cold ham, potatoes, and, at the last, oatmeal boiled in saltwater which, Devlin enlightened her, was called hasty pudding. Tankards of port wine accompanied the dinner.

As they left the dining hall, the four roisterers raised their glasses to them in salute, and when O'Reilly, the innkeeper, candle in hand, started to lead Devlin and Jane up the stairs, Jane heard them begin to sing:

"The innkeeper's daughter was a winsome sight,
  She served rare vintages every night—"
Devlin paused at the door to his room, glanced down

the stairs and then at O'Reilly. "I expect no hullabaloo tonight," he said with a warning edge to his voice.

"You may rest assured of that, milord," O'Reilly told him.

Devlin looked at Jane, starting to reach toward her, and she thought he was about to speak. Instead his hand dropped to his side and he nodded and bade her good night. She followed O'Reilly up a second flight of stairs and along a narrow hall. When he came to the end of the passage, he opened the door to a small chamber, ushering her inside, handing her the candle and mumbling a goodnight. As soon as Jane heard his departing footsteps, she slid home the bolt on the door.

She looked around her, surprised that the tiny chamber had enough room for a dresser, a commode with a water pitcher on the top, and even a wicker chair. Cunningham had placed her portmanteau on the bed.

Tired to the bone, Jane fell asleep almost at once. She awakened with a start, peering into the jet-darkness of the chamber with the shards of a dream still troubling her, a dream of naked women dancing hand-in-hand around a bonfire, of demons and witches, flying high above the earth as they followed the path of the full moon, darkly silhouetted against a shifting, slanting phantasmagoria of lights in the western sky.

Hearing raucous cries from outside the inn, she went to the window and pushed open the casement, shivering as the night air pierced the thin fabric of her cotton nightgown. She peered cautiously down into the dimly lit courtyard where she saw vague forms moving about. A man called out, another answered in anger, she heard oaths followed by the sounds of a scuffle and then other shouts and cries.

The scuffling stopped and she heard a man's voice ask, "Shall we bleed the two of them to cool their ardor?" and another answer, "The only blood to be shed this night shall be the blood of the grape." This sally was followed by laughter and cheers.

"No more of this, me buckos." Jane recognized the voice of O'Reilly, the innkeeper.

A loud outcry followed, the sound of blows and then confused cries of protest. Men shouted and cursed, she saw dark forms carrying a struggling man. "Into the trough with him," someone cried. There was a loud splash and more laughter.

Doors opened and slammed shut; footsteps thudded on the stairs, she heard a knocking on a door inside the inn but on the floor below hers. A woman shrieked with fearful delight, a man laughed huskily, suggestively, then a moment's quiet was broken by cheering. Once more the inn grew silent.

In growing alarm, Jane closed the window and hurried to the door, testing the bolt. Should she seek Devlin's help? Undecided, her heart pounding, she stood with her hand on the latch, listening. The silence was broken by the sound distant, discordant singing. The danger, she assured herself, was past.

Returning to her bed, she lay on top of the blankets and closed her eyes but, still uneasy, made no attempt to seek sleep. The singing stopped and the night was quiet once again. She sighed with relief. Now she could sleep and tomorrow, she told herself, they would drive on to Worcester, find the Reverend Miles at his brother's rectory and recover the cloak. Her cloak.

And be damned to Lord Devlin.

A stair board creaked in the hall. Jane sat up, all her senses alert, listening, heard a stealthy footfall just beyond her door. There came a tapping on the door itself. Her heart raced. Should she scream? Or remain silent? The night was quiet, the only sound in the room came from her own rapid breathing.

Again the tapping. "Betsy?" A man's slurred voice from the hall.

She said nothing, sat unmoving on the bed, her hand at her throat. This, she recalled, was Betsy's room. More tapping, louder now, more insistent. "Betsy, open the door." A loud, urgent whisper.

If she said nothing, he would leave, Jane told herself. She heard the impatient clicking of the latch followed by a muttered curse. Jane held her breath.

Another curse. Footsteps. Retreating? A loud thump as a shoulder struck the door, the wrenching crack of splintering wood, the door slamming back against the wall. She lifted the pitcher from the commode. A man's form loomed in the doorway. Footsteps crossed the room to her bed. A groping hand touched her shoulder.

Jane swung the pitcher, heard and felt the impact as it struck the intruder. She drew back the pitcher again, gasped as it was knocked from her hand to thud onto the floor. She started to scream only to feel a hand clamp over her mouth.

Six

Jane tried to twist away only to have her assailant's grip tighten over her mouth, painfully bruising her lips. She gagged, nauseated by the stench of liquor on his breath.

"Sweet Betsy," he whispered. "Shhhhh!"

Even as she shook her head to try to tell him she was not Betsy, she felt him kneel beside her on the bed, one hand covering her mouth while his other hand grasped her shoulder and then roamed downward to fondle her breast.

Desperate, she forced her mouth open and, when she felt his fingers between her teeth, bit down with all the strength at her command. She tasted the tang of blood.

"Aaugh!" Her assailant jerked back his hand.

Jane screamed.

He struck her, his hand slapping hard against the side of her face. Her breath caught as she winced in pain. Before she could move, he clutched her nightgown with both hands and tore it asunder. Cursing angrily, he gripped her upper arms, pinning her to the bed as he straddled her, looming above her in the darkness like a beast from the wild.

She saw a light gleam behind the intruder, saw a hand grasp his shoulder and yank him away to sprawl on the foot of the bed. Jane gasped, folding her arms across her breasts as she shrank back against the headboard, unsure whether the newcomer was friend or foe.

Her attacker tried to push himself up from the bed but, becoming entangled in the blankets, sprawled face down. Devlin—she saw it was Devlin who had come to her rescue—lifted the man bodily, held him over his head for a moment and then hurled him to the floor in the narrow space between the bed and the wall. The man—he was not one of the roisterers from the dining hall but someone she had never seen before—gave a strangled cry of pain.

Devlin reached down and pulled the intruder to his feet. The man flailed at him, cursing drunkenly, but Devlin pinioned one of his arms behind his back and shoved him to the doorway where, with a furious thrust, he sent him reeling along the passageway.

There was silence and then a weak voice called, "Betsy?"

Devlin strode into the hall, answering in a furious and threatening voice. A moment later she heard unsteady footsteps descending the stairs.

Devlin returned to the chamber, his face flushed, his black hair tousled and his long purple robe ripped. Retrieving his oil lamp from the floor, he came to stand beside her bed. "Are you all right?" he asked, his voice urgent with concern.

Holding her torn nightgown together with one hand, Jane drew in a deep, shuddering breath as she struggled up and sat on the edge of the bed. "I—I believe so," she said. "Yes, yes, I am."

"Thank God." After placing the lamp on the dresser, Devlin sat beside her on the bed, gently putting his arm around her.

She shivered; tears filled her eyes. "Oh, Devlin," she gasped between sobs, "I was so terribly frightened." Tears streaked her cheeks as she pressed her face against his chest. With one hand he clasped both of hers, squeezing them reassuringly, while with the other he gently stroked her shoulder, murmuring words of comfort, stroked her hair, promising her she was safe now, safe with him, telling her she had no reason to be frightened for he would stay with her and protect her.

Comforted, her sobbing lessened and her trembling finally stopped but, feeling secure within the circle of his arms, she remained nestled against him. When his fingers found the nape of her neck, tenderly caressing her bare flesh, an exquisite warmth spread throughout her body and she found herself wishing she could remain here in his arms. Forever.

No! This would never do.

Jane shook her head and pushed herself from Devlin only to have him take her by the shoulders, holding her away from him as he stared at her, his eyes glittering with a fire that alarmed her even as it kindled an answering flame deep within her, a flame of needing and of wanting, a flame of desire more compelling than any she had ever known or ever thought possible.

He held her a moment longer and then, with a heartfelt sigh, released her. Standing, he walked to the window where he stood looking into the dark night. Shaking off her bemusement, she left the bed and hurried to the chair where she picked up her robe and slipped it on.

What must Devlin think of her? Did he believe she had thrown herself into his arms because she was an adventuress bent on tempting a peer of the realm? At the very least he must consider her a typical young lady, faint of heart and in dire need of a gentleman's protection. She had promised him she would be able to fend for herself and now, less than twenty-four hours later, she had been forced to call on him for help.

Devlin turned from the window to look at her, his expression unreadable. "The Angel Inn fails to live up to its name," he said caustically.

Chilled by his studied casualness, she made no reply.

Devlin retrieved the water pitcher from the floor and returned it to the top of the commode before kneeling in front of the door to examine the shattered wood of the frame. "This bolt is useless," he told her. "Wait for me, I shall be back in a matter of minutes."

Stay with me! The cry rose to her lips but she clenched her fists and bit the words back.

"Mr. O'Reilly?" she asked instead. "Has he been harmed? I think they threw him in the watering trough."

"O'Reilly is perfectly safe except for assorted bruises. He was the one who roused me."

After Devlin left, Jane stood behind the chair holding tensely to its back, staring at the ruined door while trying to convince herself she was safe. When she heard footsteps in the hall she drew in her breath.

"Devlin here," he called and she sighed in relief. How thoughtful of him to understand and do what he could to allay her fear.

Devlin seemed to be two separate people, one the man who had comforted her and who, she suspected, cared for her more than he might be willing to admit. The other, the man who sought the King's Cloak, an enemy who resented her presence on this journey and so treated her with an arrogant coolness. She felt a growing affection for the one, a lingering antagonism toward the other.

He came in carrying two blankets under his arm. As he spread them on the floor near the foot of the bed, he said, "I intend to spend the remainder of the night here with you."

She knew she should protest, should insist she would be all right alone but she had to admit she wanted him here. But only, she told herself, because she was still upset.

"Shall I leave the lamp lit?" he asked.

When she shook her head he turned down the wick and the flame died. Still wearing her robe, she slipped into bed, drawing the blankets up to her chin. Hearing his steps, she peered into the darkness at his approach-

ing form with a tingling anticipation mingled with
trepidation.

"Sleep well," Devlin said, tucking the covers around
her shoulders. He leaned down and kissed her chastely
on the forehead.

Her throat tightened and she felt the sting of tears
as she recalled her father tucking her into bed and
kissing her good night in much the same way long,
long ago. She had had a home then. Would she ever
have one again?

She closed her eyes, listening to Devlin settling himself on the floor between the bed and the door. Sleep,
she realized, would be slow in coming, not so much
because she was still perturbed by the stranger's attack,
though she was, but more because she was so acutely
aware of Devlin's presence only a few feet from her.
He, too, seemed restless for she heard him turn this
way and that on his makeshift bed.

Once more her thoughts returned to her father and
she said softly, almost as much to herself as to Devlin,
"After my mother died when I was born, my father
was often at sea, sailing from New Orleans to New
York or Boston or South America. I saw little of him
but I worshipped him, perhaps because he was gone
so often and for so long at a time."

At first she thought Devlin was already asleep or
chose to remain silent but then he said, rather
brusquely, "I scarcely have any memory of my father,
or my mother either, when I was young, not until I
was ten or eleven. I was raised by nannies and then
educated by tutors—I suppose I believed everyone

was—before I was sent off to Harrow. After that I saw even less of my father except when I was home on holiday."

How dreadful that must have been for him, she thought, how unfair, how cruel. I would never bring up a child of mine in such an inhuman way.

"Everyone was always so kind to me when I was young," she said, "especially the Pariots. They were related to my mother in only the vaguest way and yet they took me in without so much as a murmur and treated me as one of their own even though they were barely managing to make ends meet. I always thought—"

Jane paused, realizing she had been about to tell him one of her innermost dreams, a secret she had never revealed to anyone. This day and this night, the long drive with Devlin from Lyon Hall to London and then to the Angel Inn, the turmoil followed by the stranger's drunken intrusion into her room and now this shared intimacy in her bed chamber in darkness of the early morning, all seemed to inspire the sharing of confidences.

"You always thought?" he repeated.

"That I owed recompense in return for all that was given to me when I was girl, that I was obligated to others, not only to my father and the Pariots but to all those who happened to be less fortunate than myself. I hope someday to repay the kindness of others, to help make their lives as happy as mine has been."

Jane paused, wondering what Devlin would say, whether he would scoff at her idealistic notion and inform her she was obligated to no one but herself.

She realized that his opinion, surprisingly, meant more to her than she would ever admit to anyone but especially to him.

"I never believed I owed anyone anything," Devlin said. "I fear I always accepted whatever was given me as my rightful due."

"When I received my legacy last year," Jane said, "when I learned I had inherited Lyon Hall, I thought I would soon have the wherewithal to be able to help others. Young Joshua, for instance, the stableboy you asked to care for Horatio. He happens to be an orphan like myself and a bright lad, too, by all accounts, a lad who would profit from schooling. But, alas, he can neither read nor write and most likely never will."

"Do you believe in portents?" Devlin asked as though his thoughts had veered away from what she was telling him. "In signs and omens?"

Jane shook her head only to belatedly realize he could not see her in the dark. "No," she told him, then frowned as she reconsidered. "Yes, perhaps some portents. It depends, I suppose, on what you mean by portents."

"When I was very young, aged five or six, I had the great good fortune to be taken to meet King George the Third. All I recall of the king is an impression of a resplendently garbed old gentleman—at least I considered him old at the time though he must have been little more than fifty—who took me by the hand and led me into his workroom where he showed me, with a great deal of pride, a pocket watch he was assembling. After he returned me to my father, the king placed his hand on my head as though to bless me. 'A fine lad you have here,' he said, 'England expects much of him.' I remember nothing more but I never forgot the king nor what he told me."

"And you considered the king's words a portent?" she asked, not clear as to what Devlin meant.

"In a certain sense, I did. From that day forward I believed I was someone extraordinary, a boy who had the greatest of expectations."

"An inheritance?"

"Not exactly, I never expected greater wealth or fame or a more exalted social position, not necessarily any of those, certainly not something as simple as a coup on the turf or at the gaming tables. But I knew with a certainty that an unusual destiny awaited me, that at some time in the future, I knew not when, at some place, I knew not where, I would receive a great boon or be given a marvelous opportunity, I knew not what. Do I presume too much, Jane? Do I sound as if I find too much favor with myself?"

Not knowing what to think, she hesitated, deflecting his question by asking one of her own. "Do you still believe in this unusual destiny of yours?"

"I do, I do indeed, although to date nothing at all extraordinary has happened to me." He was silent for a time. "I thought perchance," he went on, "it would occur after Harrow when I went up to Oxford but no, nothing remarkable happened while I was there."

"I always wished I had more schooling," Jane told him. "The Pariots sent me with their boys to the parish school and, liking school and doing well, I wanted to become a teacher but there was no money to spare. I often wonder if I would have been a good teacher. I rather think I would." Now she was the one, Jane thought, who was finding favor with herself.

"As for me," Devlin said, "I found the University a crashing bore, I considered the classics and Latin and Greek and rhetoric a waste of time. As a student, my only real love was history, especially ancient history."

"Ah, that explains Gibbon and his *Decline and Fall.*"

"Precisely. Even though reading Gibbon discomfits me at times because I can easily imagine England declining in the not too far-off future much as Rome did. That boorish and besotted would-be Lothario this evening, for instance, is but one sign of our decay. The Romans governed a vast empire while Rome itself grew ever more rotten, like a shiny apple decayed at the core. I hope England escapes a similar fate."

"Unlike America, in England you have a few men of great wealth and a multitude who have little or nothing. Much like France before their revolution."

"Not to put too fine a point on the matter, but you do have slaves in America, slaves who may one day rise against their masters." When she made no reply— agreeing with him, she had none to make—Devlin said, "After I left Oxford, after being offered and declining a fellowship—" He stopped and then, as though surprised, told her, "I just realized that never before have I talked like this to anyone. Odd, but there it is."

"Nor have I had anyone to confide in, not for many years. How strange."

"Strange yet I find talking to you in this way surprisingly comforting."

Jane smiled in the darkness, warmed by his words. "Did you travel after Oxford?" she asked, eager to hear more details of his life.

"I traveled," he said, "not on the Grand Tour to the Continent because of our war with France, but to Turkey and to Egypt, to Greece and to Italy. I waited from one day to the next as I journeyed from city to city, anticipating I knew not what but expecting something to happen only to be disappointed again and again. And later, when I served on the Peninsula under Wellington, I told myself, 'Surely now, in battle against the French and the Spanish, surely this is the time for that exceptional event to occur.' I did receive a wound at the very onset of the Battle of Vittoria that invalided me home but that was nothing."

She felt obligated to help others, Jane told herself, while Devlin had expectations of an event that would transform his life. She wondered if this was another of the differences between men and women, that women were more apt to want to give of themselves while men expected to receive, believed moreover that they deserved to receive. No, she chided, she was unfairly lauding herself at the expense of Devlin. After all, a reigning monarch had led him to expect something marvelous was his due.

"And now?" she asked.

"Do you mean do I still expect something out-of-the-ordinary to happen to me? I do indeed. Tomorrow, next month, next year, eventually, I have no notion when, but come it will."

"Possibly the King's Cloak will be involved," she suggested, wondering if she could beguile him into revealing his reason for seeking the cloak.

"Perhaps," he said, speaking slowly, "but more and more I begin to suspect that whatever it is will occur completely without warning, come like a bolt of lightning from out of nowhere, come when I least expect it." He was silent for so long she suspected he might have dozed off. "And what now for you, Jane?" he asked at last. "What will you do if you lose Lyon Hall? Where will you go?"

"I will *not* lose Lyon Hall," she declared with more assurance than she felt.

"But if you do?" he persisted.

"I suppose I would have to return to America, perhaps to Boston where Julia Bledsoe, my aunt-by-marriage, lives, or more likely go to New Orleans. Once there—" What would she do? she wondered. One of the Pariot brothers had wanted to marry her but, though she liked all three of them, she found the prospect no more appealing now than she had a year ago. She would always think of her unexpected suitor as a brother, not a husband.

"New Orleans," Devlin mused. "Sussex. Boston. How strange life is. A year ago you were in America while I was thousands of miles away in London, and then two days ago we met at Lyon Hall and a few

months from now we may be separated by thousands
of miles once more."

Jane closed her eyes, feeling sleep stealing up on
her. "I hope you recognize your great event when it
arrives," she said drowsily.

"Oh, have no fear," he said at once, "I shall recognize it, there can be not the slightest doubt of that."
He was silent for a while and she thought he had
drifted off to sleep as she was doing but then he murmured, "Someday."

"Someday," she echoed as sleep claimed her.

Jane woke to sunlight, not knowing at first where
she was. The memory of the night before came to her
with a rush and she sat up in bed. "Devlin?" she said.
There was no answer. Looking over the foot of the bed
she saw that Devlin and his blankets were gone.

There came a tapping. Before she could speak, the
door swung open. Jane, though still wearing her robe,
pulled the blankets up around her.

When Devlin came into the room she stared at him,
surprised to find him carrying a tray in one hand.
"Your breakfast, my lady," he said with a slight bow.
After placing the tray on her lap, he said, "Is there
anything else you wish?"

Jane looked at her two fried eggs, four slices of
ham, a generous portion of potatoes and a steaming
cup of cocoa. When she unfolded the napkin she un-
covered a single pink aster. "Why this is perfect!" she
cried, looking from the flower to Devlin.

"As perfect as the remainder of this day shall be,"
he promised.

The King's Cloak, she told herself with a twinge of disappointment, he must be thinking of the King's Cloak, not of the time they would spend together, for he expected to recover the cloak when they reached Malvern later in the day. Or was that what he had in mind? Forget the King's Cloak, she told herself, and enjoy the moment, be less suspicious of Devlin, perhaps he merely seeks to make amends for his boorish behavior during yesterday's drive.

"Thank you," she said, "for the flower and the breakfast, for everything but especially for the flower. This *will* be a perfect day."

And, she told herself as they drove north a short time later, it gave every prospect of being perfect for she sensed a new air of understanding between herself and Devlin, a comfortableness and at least the beginnings of a genuine liking, one for the other. As for that strange moment of need after he came to her rescue, no doubt it had been due to her unsettled nerves. She would forget that moment as undoubtedly he had.

Today Devlin left his book untouched; not only that, his sardonic manner had vanished, replaced by an air of ease, almost of intimacy, as he regaled her with tales of his Worthington forbears, some illustrious, some renowned, some eccentric, some, at least in the telling, slightly mad.

"Almost fifty years ago," Devlin told her, "my great-uncle Harold Worthington built a country home at Shrewsbury, a village close to the Welsh border. Harold had a most peculiar notion, some say it originated with a Gypsy fortune-teller, a belief he would escape death as long as he added a room to his house each and every year. Not only did he believe he must add a room but he insisted that each room be in a different style."

Jane glanced at him askance, wondering if he was exaggerating, but Devlin appeared perfectly serious.

"After thirty years," he went on, "the house had become such a hodge-podge it came to be known as Worthington's Folly. Everything changed during the thirty-first year for it was then that Harold had the misfortune to become enamored of a touring Italian opera singer. Madly in love, he followed her to Italy where he was wounded in a duel with the lady's husband and subsequently spurned by the lady herself. Harold returned to Shrewsbury a changed man, a beaten man. He abandoned his building plans and by the end of the following year he was dead. Of a broken heart, some said."

"Does this explain why you believe in portents?" Jane asked.

"Possibly," he said, "but there were no portents as far as I know in the life of my most famous ancestor, a gentleman who married a far-distant cousin of my grandfather. Besides being a reckless gambler and a middling poet, this gentleman wrote comedies for the London stage, one of which, *The Heiress,* proved to be a huge success some thirty years ago. His fame, however, came from another source entirely, since he was also a military man, the general who lost the Battle of Saratoga to your American troops in 1777, a battle some of your compatriots view as one of the most important in the history of warfare."

"Then his name must have been Burgoyne."

He looked at her with approval. "Yes, he was known as Gentleman Johnny Burgoyne. I never thought he deserved the blame he received for losing the American colonies. Another of my antecedents, a Mr. George Halverson, had the unfortunate distinction of being the only man in England who—" Devlin stopped suddenly to gaze from the window. "How swiftly the time has passed," he said. "We seem to be entering Malvern."

He was right, the time *had* sped by. Now they would seek out the Reverend Miles and, when they recovered the King's Cloak, she would, she hoped, learn what had been so important that Devlin had seen fit to deceive her. And, she thought ruefully, she would have to admit to him that she had been deceitful as well.

What, she wondered, would he make of that?

Seven

The chapel at Malvern, Jane discovered, was a new stone structure surmounted by a square bell tower. A small cemetery lay immediately to the rear of the church and, across an oak bordered lane from the row upon row of grey and white headstones was the manse, a square wooden building painted a gleaming white.

Frederic Miles himself answered Lord Devlin's knock. A spare, tall, balding man with a harried look, the dissenting pastor's only dissent from current fashion was a bushy black moustache that dominated his otherwise unremarkable face.

Devlin introduced himself and then Jane before asking the whereabouts of the Reverend Miles.

"My brother Richard? Off visiting the Holmeses, or so he said. Or the Grandbys, one or the other. I expect him to return within the hour."

Another delay, Jane told herself, but seemingly not a lengthy or a serious one. Anxious as she was to resolve the mystery of the cloak, she also wanted to take the first opportunity to ease her conscience by disclosing her deception to Devlin. She had come to the conclusion he deserved no less from her.

"Pray come in, come in," Frederic urged them, "it is indeed a pleasure and an honor to welcome you, Lord Devlin. And you as well, Miss Sterling."

He led them along a sparsely furnished hall, on the way quieting two little girls who were climbing in and out of a cupboard. Opening the door to the parlor, he ushered them into a parlor smelling faintly of dust and disuse, a dark and gloomy room despite its pair of windows overlooking a side porch.

After Jane and Devlin were seated, Frederic Miles opened, seemingly at random, a Bible resting on a marble-topped stand in the center of the parlor. He read the text: " 'I have seen servants upon horses, and the rich sit in a low place.' " Closing the book, he frowned.

"Pray pardon me," he said to Devlin and Jane, "but each time I enter a room containing a Bible I read whatever verse I come upon hoping to find an augur, a prophecy. In this case, or so it appears to me, this verse from Ecclesiastes has little or no significance."

"Unless," Devlin said, "we in England are about to experience our own version of the French Revolution."

"I believe in reform," Miles said, "but surely not revolution."

Jane, hearing a scrabbling noise from behind a settee near her, did her best to ignore it. She gave a start when, a moment later, something clutched at her gown. Looking down she saw a small child pulling itself to its feet by holding on to her.

Mr. Miles shook his head. "Wesley," he said, "how did you ever find your way into the parlor?"

Wesley, smiling up at Jane, paid no heed to his father.

Charmed by the boy's obvious trust, Jane reached for Wesley and lifted him into her lap where she hugged him. How soft and warm he felt, how lovable.

"Are the three children yours, sir?" Devlin asked.

"Mary and I have eleven in all and, God willing, it will be an even dozen come January."

"A regular quiverful," Devlin said. "You evidently believe in obeying the scriptural command to 'be fruitful, and multiply, and replenish the earth.' "

"I do, indeed," Miles said proudly, "and each new arrival has been welcomed as a blessing from heaven on high. As you would realize, my lord, if you had children of your own." The pastor sat on the settee and glanced from Jane, preoccupied with Wesley, to Devlin with what she thought was a question in his eyes. He must be wondering not only what brought them here to Malvern but what they were to one another.

"Miss Sterling and I are related," Devlin said, looking sternly at Jane when she raised her eyebrows at this less than accurate remark. "You should understand," Devlin went on in so rapid a manner that Jane had difficulty following him, "that Miss Sterling's grandmother on her father's side was the brother of the sister who was a niece by marriage of my own uncle, my great-uncle actually, and so you see our relationship is such as to make our traveling together without a chaperone perfectly proper."

"I do apologize," Mr. Miles said, "if I seemed curious. In so doing I violated one of my eight rules of conduct. Nine, rather, I added the ninth last month."

"And what might they be?" Devlin asked.

"They derive, for the most part, from John Wesley," the pastor told them, "and I do all in my power to observe them one and all even though my flesh is as weak as any other man's. My rules are these: I begin and end each day with God; I sleep as little as is necessary for good health; I employ all of my spare hours in helpful study; I do my best to avoid drunkards and busybodies as well as shunning idle curiosity, useless employment, and impractical knowledge; I never let a day pass without setting aside at least an hour for devotion and, finally, I avoid all manner of passion."

"I must congratulate you on an exceedingly commendable regimen," Devlin said, "though hardly one I would ever attempt to follow. I fear I would find it oppressive within a very short time."

"I quite understand," Jane said to their host, "how a life of discipline and sacrifice has an appeal. Although I doubt I could emulate your efforts, I could happily devote myself to serving a good cause."

"Precisely." Frederic Miles looked distracted at the sound of a baby crying somewhere toward the rear of the house. After the crying diminished and stopped, he said, "All of us are the children of God, thus each time we have decisions to make we should ask ourselves, 'What would He do?' and then proceed to do the same."

A rig rattled past the windows.

"Ah," Mr. Miles said, "my brother has returned even

sooner than I expected." He took Wesley from Jane's arms and placed him astride his shoulders. "Wait here, let me fetch him."

After the pastor left them, Devlin said, "You surprised me just now. Does a religious calling actually appeal to you?"

"Only the notion of working for the good of others rather than exclusively for myself."

Devlin nodded thoughtfully. Did that mean he actually agreed with her? She was about to ask when she heard footsteps approaching.

"Ah," Devlin said, rising from his chair, "now at long last we shall regain possession of the King's Cloak. I shall leave it to you to request the cloak's return since you were the one who gave it to the Reverend Miles."

The Miles brothers entered the room and, after introductions, Jane said, "Reverend Miles, it appears a grievous mistake was made the day before yesterday at Lyon Hall. Do you recall Aunt Estelle offering you a blue velvet cloak from the attic storeroom?"

"Oh, yes, I recall the cloak most clearly. Not a new cloak, indeed a very old cloak, but of good quality. I was most grateful to receive it. But there was a mistake of some sort?"

"Estelle believed the cloak to have little value but it was, in fact, the King's Cloak that has been in the Lyon family for generations."

"Oh, good gracious yes, I recall your showing me a similar cloak on display in a glass case. And I have, over the years, heard many tales of the King's Cloak. You say Miss Winward gave me this cloak in error?"

"We have reason to believe she did," Devlin told him with a touch of impatience. "If you will but return the cloak, Mr. Miles, I assure you I shall recompense you for any inconvenience this confusion has caused you."

"No matter how generous you are prepared to be, sir," the Reverend Miles said, "no amount you might offer will secure you the cloak."

Taken aback, Jane stared at him. "Surely you will right a wrong," she said.

"I have been accused of many things," Devlin told him, "but never of being a pinchpenny. I stand ready to offer you enough for the King's Cloak to buy not only cloaks but complete wardrobes for ten men."

"What I meant was," Miles said indignantly, "I would return the cloak if I had it in my possession. It so happens I do not."

Jane frowned. "Are you telling us you never took the cloak from Aunt Estelle after all?"

"No, no, you misunderstand from first to last. She did give me the cloak as you surmised and I brought it with me. I did, however, happen upon a poor, shivering busker in London that very same evening and made him a present of the cloak."

"Damnation!" Devlin cried.

"I implore you, sir," the elder Miles said, "to refrain from blasphemy."

"You say you gave the cloak to a busker in town,"

Devlin said, ignoring his host's protest. "Do you recall the man's name?"

The Reverend Miles shook his head. "I never thought to ask."

"What trade does a busker follow?" Jane wanted to know.

"A busker sings or recites in the street," Devlin told her before turning again to Richard Miles. "Surely you must recall where in London this magnificent act of charity of yours took place."

"Your sarcasm is as unwelcome as it is uncalled for," Miles said with unexpected force. "My behaving as a Christian, my emulating the good Samaritan who had compassion on a man who fell among thieves, may not please you but I remind you that I, nay, all of us, answer to a higher authority than yourself."

Devlin raised his eyebrows in exasperation. "I merely asked if you knew where this act of charity of yours took place. I was not suggesting you should forsake your Christian faith."

"Cousin Devlin," Jane said, "pray allow *me* to speak to the Reverend Miles."

Devlin started to protest but Jane silenced him by shaking her head slowly and emphatically. Turning to the Reverend Miles, she said, "Pray forgive my cousin, he has an unfortunate tendency to become overwrought with little or no provocation. Intemperance is an unfortunate family trait that, I believe, Cousin Devlin is making a sincere attempt to remedy."

Jane was surprised that Devlin, though he folded

his arms across his chest and stared at her in a speaking way, managed to hold his tongue.

"To err is human, to forgive divine," Miles said, glancing at Devlin and then edging ever so slightly away from him. "I would have no hesitation in telling *you,* Miss Sterling, precisely where I parted with the cloak.

"I would be obliged to you if you would."

"I was driving to our chapel in Spitalfields and had come to the intersection of Church Street and Brick Lane when I espied this poor busker, an old man of three score or more years, singing 'Lord Thomas and Fair Annet' as best he could while accompanying himself on what I took to be a guitar. He received a rather unsympathetic reception for his impromptu performance but whether his voice was rendered uncertain by age or by the chill of the night I could not tell. When the busker finished his song and was counting the few farthings in his hat, I gave him the cloak, informing him it was a gift from his creator and not from myself. He was most appreciative."

"I would have done the same," Jane told him, "and I suspect Cousin Devlin, if he had been in your place, would also have surrendered the cloak even though he might not admit it to us." She did not dare to so much as glance at Devlin as she spoke. "This busker, is there anything more you can tell me about him?"

Miles frowned in thought before shaking his head. "Nothing," he said, "nothing at all. As I stated, even his name is unknown to me."

"We both thank you for your help," Devlin told

Miles before looking meaningfully at Jane. "We must be quick off the mark," he told her, "so we should leave as soon as possible."

"I do so hope," Frederic Miles said to Jane, "that you and Lord Devlin will join my family this evening in our humble repast."

Seeing Devlin, who was standing behind both the Miles brothers, vigorously shake his head, Jane perversely said, "How gracious of you. The two of us would enjoy sharing dinner with you."

"We really should be on our way to London," Devlin protested.

"I insist you both spend the night with us," Frederic said.

Jane, picturing Devlin finding young members of the Miles menage under his bed or, perhaps, even in his bed, swallowed a smile. Though she would not mind accepting the offer of lodging, she could well imagine Devlin's choler if she accepted the offer. "How kind," she said, "but we cannot possibly stay the night."

"May I suggest," Devlin said to Jane, "a brief stroll before dinner. As we drove to the manse, I noticed some exceedingly old headstones in the churchyard across the way."

"A few date from the fifteenth century," Frederic Miles informed them proudly, "while others have rather unusual inscriptions. It would be my pleasure to show you some of the more interesting ones."

"I believe, brother," Richard said, "that Lord Devlin may have suggested a stroll because he wishes to have a private conversation with his cousin."

"Of course, of course, I am obtuse on occasion," Frederic said. "Dinner will be in an hour's time," he told his guests. "God willing."

Devlin waited until they had left the manse and were out of earshot before saying, "Why the devil did you accept the pastor's invitation? We should be on our way to Spitalfields at this very moment."

"I accepted out of politeness," she told him. And because I knew you wanted me to refuse, she could have added.

Devlin snorted. "And why have you suddenly taken it upon yourself to call me 'cousin'? "

"After listening to your speech to Mr. Miles describing our supposed relationship I came to the conclusion you must consider me to be your cousin. If you meant to indicate some other relationship you should have said so or, better still, simply told the truth."

Devlin swung his ebony cane at a leaf on a shrub, hitting it squarely and sending it whirling to the ground. "Many times white lies are appreciated by all concerned even when not believed. They have a way of easing awkward social situations."

Devlin pushed open the small wicket leading to the churchyard. "We shall depart directly after dinner," he told her as they strolled along a path between the stones, "and drive until we arrive in London. Once in town, I intend to leave you with my Aunt Charlotte while I search for our missing busker."

He glanced at Jane as though he expected her to protest. No, she decided, she would say nothing now, she would bide her time. But she certainly had no intention of letting Devlin place her on a convenient shelf while he recovered the cloak.

"Hearing no objection," he said, "I consider the matter settled." He raised his cane to point toward a thicket of shrubs and trees beyond the last row of stones. "Lord Thomas and the fair Annet," he said.

Seeing no connection between the song Mr. Miles had heard the busker sing and the thicket, Jane said, "Since I never heard the song, I fail to take your point."

"The song," he said, "is an old Scottish ballad, telling of two lovers, Lord Thomas and the fair Annet, who quarrel. Lord Thomas, in a towering rage and urged on by his family and friends, decides to wed another but when Annet appears at the wedding ceremony, he hurries to her side, ignoring his betrothed who, with a fury surpassing any found in Hell, stabs and kills Annet.

"Lord Thomas seizes the same dagger and plunges it into his heart. After they were buried near one another, she inside the churchyard and he without, a birch grew above his grave, a brier above hers. The ballad ends something like this:

" 'And yes they grew, and yes they twisted,' " he sang in a rich tenor voice,

" 'As they would fain be near;

And by this ye may know right well

They were two lovers dear.' "

"What a sad sad song," Jane said.

"The Scots *are* a bloodthirsty lot."

"That may be true," she said, "but if Lord Thomas had listened to his heart rather than to the advice of others, he might have found himself embracing Annet as a man embracing a woman rather than as a birch tree embracing a brier."

"Ah, but the true fault lies with his bride-to-be. She should have had the sense to resort to gentle persuasion rather than violence."

Jane sighed with exasperation. "You always seem to lay the blame for misfortunes at the feet of the fairer sex."

"If it were not for a member of the fairer sex," he said, "at this moment we would be disporting in the Garden of Eden rather than strolling in a country graveyard while contemplating a night journey to London to retrieve the King's Cloak."

The cloak, his thoughts constantly returned to the missing cloak. She wished she had never seen nor heard of the wretched cloak, it had caused nothing but trouble between them and would, she supposed, continue to do so. This, she decided, was as good a time as any to clear her conscience regarding the King's Cloak.

They left the churchyard and, with dry oak leaves crunching underfoot, walked onto a bridge that arched over a murmuring stream. Jane leaned over the stone railing and, when she looked down, saw her face, framed by her conversation bonnet, reflected from the dark waters of a quiet pool.

"Deceiver," she accused her image in the water.

"Did you speak?"

She heard Devlin come to stand beside her and a moment later she saw the reflection of his face appear beside hers as they both gazed down at the water.

Without turning to face him, Jane said, "I put a great value on honesty. Nothing is more hurtful than deceit, nothing more likely to lead to rows and worse."

"Do you refer to my white lie, Cousin?"

She shook her head. "No, not your lie, mine. And not merely a white one, I fear. The King's Cloak. I deceived you about the cloak. Not only you but Aunt Estelle as well."

"Oh?" He sounded surprised. "In what way?"

Jane sighed. "After you showed such a great interest in the cloak on the night of your arrival I took it from the case and put it in the wardrobe in the west wing attic. Then I told Estelle to give the clothes from the west wing—not the east wing—to the Reverend Miles, knowing how easily she would become confused when later I suggested I had said the east wing."

He stared at her in disbelief. "Why in the name of heaven did you do all that?"

"Because I was determined not to let you have the cloak, Devlin, no matter what. I could have hidden it where you could never find it but I decided to discover your reason for wanting the cloak so desperately. The best way to do that, or so I thought at the time, was to have the Reverend Miles take the cloak north with him and then accompany you when you drove after him."

Was there another reason for her deception? Jane wondered. Had she, without ever admitting the fact to herself, without even being aware of her true intent, wanted to prolong her time with Devlin? Two days ago she would have laughed at such a notion; now she wasn't altogether certain what her motive had been.

Taking a small pebble from the top of the stone railing, Devlin let it fall into the pool below them, causing the reflection of their faces to shatter into a roil of ripples. "I, too, have been less than candid," he told her.

Jane turned to him in anticipation. At last she would learn the truth about the cloak.

"I admit I gave you the impression," Devlin went on, "that I came to Lyon Hall by chance but such was not the case. When Napoleon fled to Elba earlier this year and our soldiers occupied Paris, they searched the government archives and, among other valuable documents, happened upon the diary of a seventeenth-century English gentleman by the name of Merriweather. The diary suggested that King Charles's cloak, King Charles the First, not the Second, had been entrusted to Merriweather in London and that Merriweather had hidden it somewhere along the route of his escape to France.

"A friend of mine in Whitehall asked me to try to find the cloak and return it to its rightful owner, the Prince Regent. When I heard of the so-called 'King's Cloak' at Lyon Hall in Sussex I also was informed, or, more accurately, I was misinformed, that the owners of the Hall refused to allow anyone to so much as view their treasure, let alone examine it. Therefore I invented a coaching accident to gain entry to the Hall so I would have been able to find out whether the cloak was genuine or a hoax before making an offer to purchase it. So you see, I did deceive you, and I most humbly beg your forgiveness."

Such an elaborate scheme, Jane thought, merely to

gain access to Lyon Hall. Also an unnecessary one since she would have been more than willing to show the cloak to Devlin or to any other visitor.

"You do forgive me as I forgive you?" he asked when she said nothing.

"Of course I forgive you," she told him.

"And so," Devlin said as they walked down from the arch of the bridge and started back to the manse, "we have both made our confessions and the air is now clear between us."

But was it? Jane wondered, casting him a sideways look. She had a nagging suspicion that Devlin had told her only a portion of the truth, leaving a great deal unsaid including his true reason for wanting the King's Cloak. She would, she vowed, discover the entire truth in London if, of course, they were able to find the busker and recover the cloak from him.

Or would she? Devlin proposed to leave her in the care of his aunt while he searched Spitalfields for the busker; how could she object to such an arrangement? At Lyon Hall she had been able to threaten him with M. LaSalle but the Frenchman was now many miles away. In London, Devlin would be able to enforce the ironclad rules of society and strand her with his aunt.

Since she could not reasonably insist on accompanying him, she was left with but one choice. She *must* find a way to retrieve the cloak without Devlin's help or knowledge. But how?

Eight

Devlin awoke, sat up and looked from the coach window to see the morning sun throwing long shadows across Old Burlington Street. They were in front of Aunt Charlotte's town house; Devlin decided that Cunningham stopping the landau must have roused him.

Jane lay curled on the seat across from him, her eyes closed, her lips slightly and very temptingly parted, a stray curl of auburn hair tumbled onto her forehead. She still wore her blue redingote and the conversation bonnet, a poke bonnet with one long and one short side. Ridiculous as he felt the bonnet to be, it failed to detract one iota from her charm, in fact, looking at her filled him with delight. He would be content, he realized, to spend the rest of the day—nay, longer, much longer—sitting here admiring the color of her russet hair, the tilt of her nose and the pink bloom of her cheeks.

The carriage door opened and, when he saw Cunningham looking up expectantly at him, Devlin reluctantly quelled his impulse to lift Jane into his arms and carry her from the carriage into his aunt's house. He sighed; this was not the day to give in to impulses no matter how inviting the prospect of holding her close might be.

Duty came before pleasure; today he must search for the King's Cloak.

Leaning to Jane, he spoke her name softly and she stirred without waking. "Jane," he said again.

Her eyes opened. For a moment she stared at him in confusion and then she offered a smile that lodged in his heart. Almost immediately her smile faded and she asked, "Where are we?"

"We have just arrived at my Aunt Charlotte's town house," he told her. "On Old Burlington Street."

She sat up, hastily straightening her bonnet and smoothing her coat. "I must look a fright," she said.

"On the contrary, you look astonishingly fetching," he assured her as he handed her down from the carriage. It was no more than the truth. Once she had alighted, he found it exceedingly difficult to let go of her hand.

"What will your aunt think when we appear out of nowhere in the early hours of the morning?" Jane asked. "What will she think of me? She, at least, must know you cannot claim me as a cousin."

"Lottie always expects the unexpected from me," Devlin said as he escorted her up the front steps and pulled the bell chain. "I have a suspicion she favors me for that very reason." The door opened and Devlin said, "Ah, Arnold, if you will tell my Aunt Charlotte her favorite nephew has arrived to pay a call."

As Devlin thought likely, Arnold appeared not the least bit surprised at their unexpected arrival. With his customary aplomb, the butler showed them into the drawing room before leaving to summon his mistress.

Noticing Jane looking up at a gilt-framed portrait over the fireplace, Devlin said, "That, Jane, is the General. He actually was my Uncle Chauncey but I always thought of him as the General." He smiled. "There were those, myself included, who thought Lottie should have been made the general rather than Chauncey. He died of a fall from a horse three years ago leaving Aunt Charlotte both grieving and exceedingly plump in the pocket."

"Not as plump in the pocket as you seem to believe, Charles." A woman who Devlin always thought must appear formidable to strangers—she was tall, statuesque, and handsome—bore down on them. "And, you might have informed the young lady that you are not only my favorite nephew but my *only* one."

"If you had a dozen or more," Devlin said, "I would still expect to be your favorite." He looked from Jane to his aunt. "Aunt Charlotte," he said, "may I present Miss Jane Sterling of Lyon Hall, Sussex."

"I never stand on ceremony," Devlin's aunt said, "so I shall call you Jane and you must call me Charlotte."

"Could I impose on your good nature?" Devlin asked his aunt after a brief exchange of pleasantries. "Could Jane—Miss Sterling—stay here as your house guest for a few days?"

Charlotte looked from Devlin to Jane and back to Devlin. "Of course she may," she said, smiling at Jane. "Now do tell me what brings you to town, Charles."

"Really too involved a story. Later, allow me to explain later. I must be on my way at once." He tried to think of something that might satisfy his aunt's curiosity without requiring a lengthy explanation. "Miss Sterling is an American," he said to distract her.

What did Lottie think of Americans? he wondered. He wanted her to like Jane; in fact he suddenly realized it was terribly important to him that she both liked and approved of Jane. "With English antecedents," he added hastily. "She inherited Lyon Hall only six months ago."

"In Sussex, I believe you said. Did you drive from there this morning?"

Devlin glanced down at his wrinkled clothing, all at once realizing how disheveled he must appear. He looked at Jane, trying, with little success, to see her through another's eyes rather than his own. She *did* appear tired, he should have been aware of that; her coat and gown were wrinkled. He had been so captivated by *her* rather than what she wore that he had failed to notice.

"Drive to town from Lyon Hall?" he said to Charlotte. "No, we drove from Malvern. Left there after dinner last night."

"Malvern!" Charlotte frowned at Devlin and then touched Jane lightly on the sleeve. "I often wonder what goes through my nephew's mind. You must be exhausted, my dear, let me show you to your room and send Maud to help you. As for you, my favorite nephew"—she turned to Devlin—"I shall expect a full explanation when I come down."

Devlin shook his head. "Later today, perhaps tomorrow," he told her, edging toward the door, preparing to flee his aunt's curiosity. No, Jane deserved better from him, he thought; he would not, could not, leave her without a word. "When I recover the cloak," he said to Jane, "I shall bring it here forthwith."

"The cloak?" Charlotte asked. "Another riddle! What cloak is that?"

"I shall explain all upon my return," Devlin promised.

He began to turn on his heel only to abruptly change his mind. Striding to Jane, he lifted her hand to his lips, looked into her green eyes and, for a timeless moment, seemed to fall into their fathomless depths. He started to speak, failed to find the right words, finally turned and left the drawing room. Had he ever been so confused in his life? he wondered as he hurried from the house. He must be more tired than he thought to behave in such a befuddled manner. What must Lottie think of him?

After stopping briefly at his town house, Devlin drove east toward Spitalfields. Jane wanted to find the cloak before he did, or so he strongly suspected, but he had successfully forestalled her by leaving her with Lottie. Jane might be cleverer than most women and she might be as resourceful as many men, but she was not a conjuror able to make the King's Cloak appear with the wave of a wand.

He would find the cloak.

Or would he?

As he drove through the crowded streets of London the enormity of his task became clear to him. He sought one man among more than a million souls, a shadowy figure he thought of as the Unknown. What was the Unknown's name? He had not the slightest notion. Where did he live? In Spitalfields or in some other part of town? Perhaps the Unknown was only passing through London; if so, the chances of finding him were small indeed.

The Unknown was a busker, he did know that, a singer of songs. But there must be hundreds of street singers in London, both those who earned a pittance from their singing and those who were otherwise employed but sang for the love of singing. Wherever one went in town, he recollected with dismay, one heard songs being whistled by passersby or played on barrel organs in the streets or sung in tap-rooms.

The Reverend Miles, good Samaritan that he was, had given the cloak to the Unknown near the intersection of Brick and Church Streets and so, hoping it might be a favorite haunt of the busker, that was where he was bound. As his landau pounded over the cobbles, he drove past taverns and chop houses, tobacco shops displaying theatre playbills and eating houses promising fourpenny and sixpenny plates, penny bread and penny potatoes. Pouring over the problem of locating the cloak, he half-heard the chiming of church clocks, the barking of dogs, and the thrum of the traffic in the streets.

They soon arrived in Spitalfields, for many years a silk weaving center, once prosperous but now in sad decline with unpaved streets, open sewers, and old mansions changed into overcrowded tenements. Leaving Cunningham with the carriage on Brick Street, Devlin began his search on foot.

Three hours later the Unknown was still the Unknown. No one recollected seeing or hearing him, no one at all; seemingly the busker had disappeared into the city's fetid air taking the King's Cloak with him. For one man to find the busker among the city's innumerable streets and alleys was, Devlin realized belatedly, well-nigh impossible.

Fortunately, he could ask for help in his search, in this case the help of Mr. Arthur Ackroyd. He had wanted to find the cloak himself, without assistance of any sort, but a wise man, he reasoned, knows when to swallow his pride and admit he needs help. That time had come.

"To Whitehall," he ordered Cunningham when he returned to the carriage, well aware his coachman knew exactly where he wanted to go.

Within the hour Devlin was sitting in a leather armchair facing Mr. Arthur Ackroyd, a friend since his first day at Harrow, across a disordered desk. Ackroyd, pink-faced and rotund, was slouching in his chair, resembling, Devlin thought, a Cruikshank portrait depicting Lethargy and Sloth. Ackroyd's cluttered desk and nondescript quarters in an otherwise impressive government building suggested an abysmal lack of efficiency.

These impressions, Devlin knew, were completely false. He had often suspected that Ackroyd carefully cultivated an air of indolence so his subsequent actions, which were more often than not both bold and sweeping, would seem even more enterprising than they actually were. To Devlin's way of thinking, if Ackroyd had a fault it was a tendency to act hastily, often without a judicious weighing of the possible consequences.

Ackroyd gestured lazily toward a stack of papers on his desk. "I read your report," he told Devlin. "Well written, as always, concise and literate yet all-inclusive. Sussex, Lyon Hall, the King's Cloak, all that. I believe you mentioned the presence of a Frenchman in the neighborhood. May I offer a word of warning?"

"About M. Claude LaSalle?"

"Claude LaSalle, yes. I thought I recognized the name so I asked Harper to make a search of our files. Without results as yet, I regret to say. Be wary, however, of this M. Claude LaSalle."

"I shall indeed," Devlin promised. "I suspected he was a rogue from the first."

"Now then," Ackroyd said, "what news have you to report?"

"I had great hopes that the Reverend Miles would have the cloak in his possession but, alas, he had given it to a busker while passing through Spitalfields."

Ackroyd nodded, steepling his hands and listening without comment while Devlin told of his unsuccessful foray to Malvern and his more recent search for the busker in Spitalfields. "So now," Devlin concluded, "having come a-cropper, I turn to you."

"Are you fairly certain," Ackroyd said, "that this cloak is the one we want? The one mentioned in Merriweather's journal?"

"I would wager three to one it is. No, more, five to one."

"As you are aware," Ackroyd said, gesturing vaguely in the direction of Carlton House, *"he* has more than a passing interest in the recovery of the cloak."

Devlin nodded, knowing the emphasized "he" referred to none other than the Prince Regent.

"Also allow me to remind you," Ackroyd said, "that you are to let no one know the reason for your interest in the cloak. This particularly applies to possible enemies of Britain such as the Americans and the French. The Prince has enough difficulties in Parliament as it is because of the expense of maintaining Carlton House and his pavilion at Brighton."

"You may rest assured," Devlin said, "that I shall tell no one why I seek the cloak."

"Excellent. To help you recover the cloak I intend to immediately call on the Charleys for help which is quite appropriate since they were named for King Charles. And your given name is Charles as well—a good omen. The Charleys, together with at least twenty men from this office, will scour all of London for this missing busker of yours. If this fails—I doubt it will— I plan to enlist the support of the army."

"I knew I could depend on you, Arthur," Devlin said. "Of course I intend to keep searching myself."

Ackroyd left his chair, walked to the window and looked out over a fog-shrouded London. "We shall not flag or fail," he said in the cadenced tones of an orator. "Our search shall go on to the end. We shall seek this elusive busker in Spitalfields, we shall seek

him in Vauxhall Gardens and in Soho, we shall seek
him in Lambeth and in Covent Garden, in Mayfair
and Kensington. And, before this week is out, we
shall have him and, more importantly, we shall have
the King's Cloak."

"I can ask for no more," Devlin told him.

"And Charles agreed to have you accompany him
to Malvern to seek this King's Cloak of yours?" Charlotte asked Jane later that afternoon as they strolled in
the walled garden at the rear of her town house.

"Not at first. In fact he objected most strenuously.
He only agreed, and then most reluctantly, when I
threatened to seek the assistance of a neighbor, a
Frenchman, one M. LaSalle."

"Good for you," Charlotte said. "Charles needs a
comeuppance now and again. Though a splendid young
man in many ways, he tends to be a bit too high in the
instep. A firm set down does him the world of good."

Jane nodded. She was, she found, becoming accustomed to Charlotte's outspokenness. At first she had
been taken aback by the older woman's candor but the
longer she was with Charlotte the more she liked her.
Though given to voicing strong opinions, Charlotte
also had the courtesy to listen to the views of others
and the good sense to change her position when shown
to be wrong.

"Do you find him rather insufferable?" Charlotte
asked with a sidelong glance. "I suspect you do."

Reluctant to criticize Charlotte's only nephew, Jane hesitated before admitting, "At times."

Charlotte smiled. "And are you in love with him?" she asked.

Jane looked away to conceal her vivid flush. Do I love Devlin? she asked herself. What a ludicrous notion! About to reply with a sharp "Certainly not," she hesitated, suddenly at sea as she recalled her confused response when he kissed her in the west attic, her sudden flare of need when he held her in his arms at the Angel Inn. What *were* her feelings for Devlin?

"I *do* beg your pardon," Charlotte said. "Such a thoughtless question. Sometimes my curiosity quite overwhelms my good manners." She stooped and plucked a deep russet bloom from a bush laden with showy, many-petaled flowers. "Have you ever seen such a heavenly color?" she asked.

Relieved by the change of subject, Jane shook her head. "Nor have I seen that particular flower before," she said. "Nor smelled such a strangely exotic scent."

"They call it a chrysanthemum," Charlotte told her, "a plant recently brought to Britain from China. How amazingly well it goes with your hair," she said, handing the russet flower to Jane.

They walked on, pausing beneath an arbor where, in the spring, roses must have bloomed in profusion. "I do so worry about Charles," Charlotte said. "Men and women have seasons much as flowers do. At a certain time of life, men should marry; I do believe Charles has reached that time."

Jane, uncomfortable, made no reply. Devlin, she was

convinced, had given little or no thought to the possi
bility of marriage. And whether he had or not wa
certainly no concern of hers.

"When a gentleman's season for marrying passe
him by," Charlotte said, "he either remains a bachelo
and slowly withers, dries up, and is blown away by
the wind or else he weds late in life, usually lured into
wedlock by a conniving young lady half his age whose
interest in him is more financial than affectionate."

"And if he marries too soon?" Jane asked, interested
in Charlotte's notions in spite of herself.

"A young man, lacking experience with both women
and life, is apt to be captivated by such trivial attribute
as a young lady's charming smile or her gift for laughte
or because she happens to be all the rage with othe
gentlemen or, and this is much more practical even
though almost as foolish, her expectations. 'Married in
haste, we may repent at leisure.' "

"Is it possible that marriage is for women but no
for men?"

"No, I think not, for almost all men *should* marry
A married man is likely to be happier than a bachelo
He has children and grandchildren to add interest to hi
old age rather than having to depend on dogs. And,
do believe, a married man lives longer. Charles, in par
ticular, should marry before much more time elapses
Unfortunately, he seems to find the young ladies of the
ton rather boring. Not that I can say I disagree with
him."

"Surely there must be someone for him," Jane said

Charlotte gave Jane an appraising look. "I quit

concur," she said as they left the arbor, "although that someone may very well not be of the *ton.*" She stopped to pick a small bouquet of chrysanthemums.

"Has Maud proven satisfactory?" she asked as she straightened with the flowers in her hand. "Though an excellent seamstress, she never served as a lady's maid before."

Jane hesitated, then, deciding truth was always best, replied, "I confess to not being accustomed to having a personal maid. Maud does well enough though she cries and sobs a great deal."

Charlotte nodded. "The girl is a regular watering pot," she said.

"Is something troubling her?"

"The trouble men all too often bring to women, I fear. Maud had been walking out with a sailor, now on his way to the Orient, leaving the poor girl not only unmarried and deserted but in the family way. She insists her father would 'curse her from his door' if she returned to her home in the country and I shrink from turning her into the streets, but how can I possibly keep the girl on here?"

"Maud must come to Lyon Hall," Jane said impulsively.

"With you?" Charlotte asked doubtfully.

"No one will know her in Sussex so she can be accepted by my small staff as a widow whose husband was lost at sea. Which, in a sense, he was."

"My dear, what a generous heart you have," Charlotte said. "You have lifted a weight from my mind. As for Maud, she can begin to repay your generosity by running you up some new gowns. She really is talented in that way."

Jane nodded, knowing her gowns were sadly out of fashion.

"Now tell me more about this missing cloak of yours," Charlotte said as they began to walk back to the house, "the details of your search and whatever you know of the busker from Spitalfields."

Jane described the cloak, told of the drive to Malvern, omitting only the uproar at the Angel Inn, and related all she recalled of the Reverend Miles's account of his act of charity. She might, Jane thought hopefully, be able to enlist Charlotte's aid in finding the cloak. After a moment's reflection, she sighed in despair. Even if Charlotte agreed to help her, how could they possibly find the cloak before Devlin did?

When Jane finished, Charlotte said, "This Frenchman, this M. LaSalle, what is he like?"

"Handsome and charming." Jane paused. "And yet I find something about him disturbing. He seems insinuating, I can think of no other word. I would never have asked his help despite what I told Devlin since I cannot help but distrust him."

"From what you told me, you distrust my nephew as well."

"True." She pondered the difference between the two men. "But Devlin seems to be an honorable man who thought he was obliged to deceive me. I suspect M. LaSalle would practice deceit for its own sake."

Charlotte nodded but rather than commenting she

said, "Pray allow me to show you the General's war room."

She led Jane up the stairs and along a corridor, ushering her into to a small windowless room at the side of the house. The walls were covered with topographical maps replete with circles, squares, dotted lines, tiny flag-pins and swooping arrows.

"This is where the General came to re-fight his battles," Charlotte said. "How well I recollect the long hours I spent here, many more than I care to remember, listening to his amazingly detailed reminiscences of battlefield tactics, cavalry charges, reinforcements usually late in arriving, logistical problems, successes not fully exploited, weak right flanks and retreats that unfortunately turned into routs."

Jane frowned, puzzled as to why Charlotte had brought her here. "Are you wondering," she ventured at last, "what tactics the General would employ if he were searching for the busker?"

"Exactly," Charlotte said.

"So we can do the same?"

"Not at all. Since most men think alike, knowing what the General would have done will tell me what Charles and his cohorts are likely to do. You did say he stopped at Whitehall on the way to Malvern?"

"Yes, very briefly. A matter of only a few minutes."

"Time enough, however, to submit a report. He has friends there. As a matter of fact, when Charles journeyed to Paris shortly after Napoleon's defeat I wondered if he went merely as a tourist or whether he was acting for our government in some way."

Could Devlin be acting on behalf of Britain? Jane asked herself. Was that why he had been so ready to deceive her?

Charlotte clasped her hands and closed her eyes. "Yes," she said, opening her eyes after a few minutes of silence, "I think I know what they will do. Men think in terms of sport, of hunting, and of warfare. In this case they will view the busker as a fox and they will start a grand hunt for him with much tallyhoing, using scores of men to track him to his lair."

"That sounds reasonable," Jane said.

"Eminently so. And what would you do, Jane, if you were in the busker's place and found yourself the object of such a hunt?"

Jane had no need to ponder the question. "I would do exactly what the fox does—run as fast as I could looking to go to cover."

"Which is what the busker will do as soon as the hounds of Whitehall are in full cry which, I suspect, will be tomorrow at the latest. The hounds might succeed, I grant you that, and Charles may find his quarry. On the other hand, he may never find him and this King's Cloak of yours will be lost forever."

"True enough," Jane said, "but is there anything *we* can do?"

"I believe there is." Charlotte nodded. "Yes, there is a way to steal a march on Charles." After glancing from side to side as though afraid of eavesdroppers, she leaned toward Jane, lowering her voice. "Listen to my scheme for recovering the cloak," she said, "and tell me what you think."

Nine

A fog settled over London during the night. When Devlin returned to Spitalfields the next morning, the sun shone weakly through the soot-darkened shroud over his head. The damp air seemed heavy and oppressive, carriages and carts rattled slowly over the cobbled streets, many led by torch-bearing men, and passersby reminded him of wraiths as they appeared from out of the mist only to be swallowed up again behind the yellowish veil of the fog.

Though by nature an optimist who perceived possibilities where others saw only difficulties, Devlin soon began to become discouraged. The chance that he or anyone else would find the Unknown on such a day as this appeared remote indeed. He had never won a wager at odds of greater than forty to one; the odds against his success today appeared to be at least twice that daunting figure.

He was determined, however, to continue the search, vowing to do his best, come what may.

Cane in hand, he started walking toward the south and west, making his way slowly in the direction of the river, but almost at once he found himself lost in a rabbit-warren of haphazard streets and alleys. After a considerable time he turned a corner and, without warning, the soaring dome of St. Paul's loomed above him and he drew in his breath, astonished as he always was by the beauty of Christopher Wren's cathedral. Within minutes, though, he was lost again with only the dank odor of the river telling him he was nearing the Thames.

He skirted around an outdoor market where women shuffled among stalls that offered, as far as Devlin could see in the gloom, little more than potatoes and apples. As he walked on along ever narrower streets, he wrinkled his nose as he breathed air made fetid by sewage running in the gutters. He heard babies crying, the barking of a dog, the slow rumble of an unseen cart, the angry shouts of a man, all mingling with the chiming of bells as each church in turn insisted that it and it alone was privy to the correct time of day.

The sound of male voices raised in song came faintly from out of the fog ahead of him. Hopeful, Devlin quickened his pace, guided by a pale glow. He soon recognized the song as a ribald sea chantey, the diffused glow became the many-paned window of a gin shop. A faded sign extending outward above the door told him he was nearing the threshold of "The Albatross."

Devlin pushed open the door and was greeted by an inviting warmth uninvitingly tinged with the stench of sweat and gin. The singing stopped abruptly as all eyes peered through the haze of smoke at this newly arrived intruder from another world. There were perhaps nine men in the small room, Devlin guessed, leather-faced, tattooed men in heavy woolens, some bareheaded, others wearing tasseled knit hats, hard cases one and all, men who viewed Devlin with short-fused suspicion ready to explode into hostility.

"A busker?" a seaman said, repeating Devlin's question. "Ain't seen no buskers hereabouts." The answer was confirmed by a general shaking of heads.

Devlin hesitated, considering whether to buy drinks for all, but decided against it. Leave bad enough alone, he cautioned himself. With a thanks and a lifting of his cane in a farewell salute, he left the gin shop and strode away into the fog.

He came upon the boy so suddenly he collided with him. Only by grasping the boy's arm—in doing so Devlin dropped his cane—did he keep the youngster from hurtling backward onto the pavement.

"I *am* sorry," Devlin said. "The fog—"

The lad, red-haired and pathetically thin, stared up at him with a fear born of experience etched on his face. He was, Devlin thought, eight or nine years old. When Devlin picked up his cane but made no move to raise it in anger, the boy's look of fear changed to one of cunning.

As Devlin warily watched, the boy reached into a pocket of his shabby oversized coat and brought forth an undersized apple. Clutching the apple firmly in one hand, he held it up for Devlin's inspection. It looked, Devlin realized, much like the apples he had seen a short while before in the outdoor market.

"Penny for the apple," the boy said.

"A penny!" Devlin cried, feigning shock. "Merely a penny for that magnificent fruit?"

The boy gaped at him, eyes darting this way and that as though he was undecided whether to run or stand his ground. He stood his ground.

Devlin tossed the boy a shilling. The boy caught the silver coin and stared at it in happy surprise.

"The apple," Devlin reminded him.

The boy handed him the apple, turned as though to run, looked back at Devlin and then edged away into the fog as though reluctant to see the last of this unexpected benefactor.

Picking up his cane, Devlin walked slowly on, musing to himself. He realized he had been taken with the boy even while suspecting him of being little more than a thief; he wondered why. Could it have been the lad's hair, the red shade reminding him of Jane? He had never given children much thought, considering them rather a nuisance, but in the last few days, when he had seen a few of Pastor Miles's quiverful and now encountering this street arab, he began to wonder if he might have been hasty in his judgment.

Hearing footsteps behind him, Devlin stopped and turned, half expecting to find that the lad had followed him. When the footsteps also stopped, Devlin, after a moment's hesitation, walked on but once more heard the padding of shoes on the pavement behind him. Again he stopped and turned.

A man appeared out of the fog; Devlin recognized him as one of the seamen from *The Albatross*. The seaman swept his cap from his head and stood holding

t in his hands. "You was lookin' for a busker?" he
sked.

"I was." Devlin, suspicious, tightened his grip on
is cane.

"The busker, 'e lives down that lane. There." The
eaman pointed to a dark alleyway. "Leyland Lane,"
e added.

Devlin said nothing, waiting for the seaman to ask
or money but, unexpectedly, he touched his cap,
urned, and without a backward glance, disappeared
nto the fog. Devlin stood listening, not knowing what,
f anything, to expect, but heard only distant street
ounds muted by the fog. Finally he walked slowly to
he entrance of the alley, peering into the yellow-grey
loom, seeing nothing. He took a few tentative steps,
ane held at his side, the stones wet and slippery under
is feet. Barrels had been piled against a brick wall
o his right, a short distance beyond the barrels he saw
a dark doorway.

He drew in a deep breath. In for a penny, he told
imself, walking ahead.

He glimpsed something. Too late. Strong hands
eized his arms, his cane clattered to the stones. A
man loomed in front of him, a stave in his upraised
and. Devlin shouted, twisting in a vain attempt to free
imself, saw the stave descending, jerked to one side,
elt a stinging blow land on his shoulder. Devlin kicked
with all his might, his booted foot striking his assailant
in the groin. He nodded with satisfaction when he
heard the man's scream.

The two men holding him pulled him backward,

tripping him; he thudded to the ground, the grip or
his arms relaxing as fingers rummaged through his
pockets. He yanked free, scrambled to his feet and
backed away. Seeing a form approach through the fog,
he lashed out, wincing with pain as his fist struck his
attacker's jaw.

Devlin's breath caught as he saw the man he had
kicked stalking him with a knife in his hand, muttering
curses as he slowly advanced. Devlin backed away
only to see his other two attackers fanning out as they
stalked him, one on each side. The time had come,
Devlin decided, to beat a hasty retreat.

Swinging around, he stumbled into one of the stacked
barrels, put out his hand to keep himself from falling
and discovered he faced a brick wall. Which way to
turn?

There came a tugging at his coat. Looking down
and behind him he saw the red-haired boy. "This way!"
the boy whispered, starting off while motioning Devlin
to follow.

For an instant Devlin hesitated, then strode after the
boy and in a few minutes they were swallowed by the
fog. The boy hurried on, undeterred either by the fog
or the maze of narrow streets and alleys, finally stopping when they reached a thoroughfare.

"White Chapel Road," the boy told him.

Devlin, realizing he was now but a few blocks from
his carriage, reached into his pocket for a coin to reward the boy for his timely help. "Damnation," he
said, finding his purse gone. "They stole my purse and

ith it all my ready," he told the boy. His cane, he realized, was also lost forever.

The boy glanced up at him with the hard look of suspicion in his eyes.

"Tell me your name," Devlin said.

The boy shuffled his feet. "Tommy Boggs," he said at last as though the name, perhaps his only possession, was somehow precious to him.

"Come with me, Tommy," Devlin told him. "Allow me to take you to my aunt to receive your reward and something to eat as well. Will you come with me?" Going to Lottie's instead of his own town house would give him the perfect opportunity, Devlin told himself, to find out how Jane was faring.

Tommy stood with his cap in his hand, his gaze fixed on the ground. Finally he shrugged.

"After you eat your fill I shall have you driven home," Devlin promised.

"Ain't got a proper home," the boy muttered. "No-where."

Devlin blinked, realizing that, though Tommy's speech was far from perfect, it was better than might be expected from a street urchin.

"In that case," Devlin said, "I shall take you wherever you wish to go. You have but to name the place."

Jane had risen early that morning only to find that Charlotte, having risen even earlier, had already eaten. When she joined the older woman in the drawing room, Jane asked, "Has anyone come? Anyone at all?"

Charlotte shook her head. "No one, though it is still early. And there *is* the fog."

Jane, restless, walked to the window and looked out at the gloom of the foggy November morning. Old Burlington Street was deserted, the houses across the way mere grey shadows, the sun, bracketed between two chimneys, appeared diminished and without warmth. The day gave every promise of being long and lonely. Despite her vow not to let him occupy her thoughts, she wondered where Devlin was at this moment, what he was doing.

"The fog may lift by afternoon," Charlotte said hopefully. "It often does, you know. And the fog will surely benefit us by impeding Charles's search for the King's Cloak."

Jane left the window to sit across from Charlotte under the watchful eye of the General. "I wish I had never heard of the King's Cloak," she said.

"But you did hear of cloak and now must make the best of it." Charlotte raised her head, listening. "Did I hear the bell?" she asked.

"I believe it *was* the bell," Jane said, looking toward the drawing-room door.

She waited, expectant though refusing to allow her hopes to rise too high.

Travis appeared in the doorway. "A busker has arrived, madam," he said to Charlotte. "As you requested, I have shown him into the music room."

"Thank you, Travis," Charlotte said. As soon as the butler left, she clapped her hands gleefully. "He could be the one," she said.

"Dare we hope?" Jane asked. Going to Charlotte, she grasped the other woman's hands. "You were right," she said, "your scheme is working."

Charlotte squeezed Jane's hands before releasing them; rising, she smoothed her skirt. "We must hope so although one busker does not a King's Cloak make. Shall we go to the music room and see what our net has pulled in?"

The busker sprang to his feet when they entered the room, bobbing his head at each of them in turn. He was, Jane saw with a shock of disappointment, exceedingly young, hardly the older street singer the Reverend Miles had described. But it might be possible that Mr. Miles had been mistaken about the man's age.

"How good of you to come at such an early hour," Charlotte told him.

"Mr. Robert Trebor at your service," the busker said, making a deep bow. "Robert Trebor is my professional name, of course, an easy name to recollect, spell Robert Trebor forward or spell it backward, the result's the same."

"How amazingly clever," Charlotte told him. "Now I must tell you at once, Mr. Trebor, we require a busker familiar with the song 'Lord Thomas and Fair Annet.' Does that ballad happen to be in your repertoire?"

Trebor shook his head. "I'm a quick study, though, I am," he said, "with the ability to master forty stanzas of any song in a matter of minutes."

Charlotte glanced at Jane who shook her head. Mr.

Trebor was positively not the man described by the Reverend Miles.

"I feel certain you could learn the song in no time at all," Charlotte told him, "but we really must have someone who already knows the song. If you will see Travis"—she nodded toward the hallway—"you will receive recompense for your trouble."

After Trebor left the room, Jane asked, "What will Travis give him?"

"A crisp one pound note. Mr. Trebor should have no cause to complain about his treatment here." When Jane started to protest the expense, Charlotte held up her hand. "You shall repay me when you have the means," she said. "This is not, I assure you, charity." Turning away from Jane, she murmured enigmatically, "I *do* have my reasons for helping you."

There was a discreet tapping at the door. "Madam," Travis said, "there are three more gentlemen in the entry hall claiming to be buskers."

Jane's hopes rose once more.

"We shall see them one at a time," Charlotte told the butler.

The first two buskers, neither of whom was able to sing 'Lord Thomas and Fair Annet' from memory, were soon sent on their way clutching their pound notes. The third, a greying gentleman who had obviously seen better days, claimed knowledge of the song.

Jane sat at the pianoforte and began to play.

"Lord Thomas and fair Annet," the busker sang,
"Sat one day on a hill.
When night had come, and sun was set,

They had not talked their fill."

"Admirably done," Charlotte said, stopping the street singer as he began the second stanza. "Now, sir, there is one other requirement you must meet in order to fill the vacancy."

The busker took a rolled newspaper page from his pocket and held it up in front of him. "The advertisement said nothing of requirements," he protested.

"Be that as it may," Charlotte told him, "the fact is the position is well-paid and so we must be extremely particular as to the qualifications of the man who fills it. You have met the first requirement; the second requirement is having a blue velvet cloak in your possession. Do you own such a garment?"

"A blue cloak?" The busker sounded flabbergasted. "I do not, though I expect I could come by a blue cloak," he said uncertainly.

"I regret to have to tell you," Charlotte said, shaking her head, "the singer must have the cloak in his possession. Pray speak to Travis on your way out to receive a little something for your time and trouble."

The busker left, muttering to himself. "A blue cloak?" Jane heard him say.

Travis reappeared in the doorway. "Madam," he said, "if you would but come into the drawing room for a moment. I never saw the like."

"Oh?" Charlotte, obviously puzzled, led Jane across the hall to the drawing room.

"If you will but look from the window," Travis said.

Jane gasped as she gazed down at Old Burlington Street. Men were everywhere, crowding the steps leading to the entrance to the house, thronging the walkway in front where they pushed against the iron fence guarding the area on one side and spilled over into the street on the other. Some were young, some old, a few carried musical instruments while others held folded copies of newspapers. Never before had she witnessed such a desperate crush.

"We almost have an embarrassment of buskers," Charlotte said, "and so we must organize our resources before we become overwhelmed. Travis, you must ask each busker whether he can sing 'Lord Thomas and Fair Annet,' sending only those who are familiar with the song either to me in the music room or to Jane here in the drawing room. You and I, Jane, will make certain they do know the song and then inquire about the cloak. Are we agreed?" Hardly pausing for answers, she hurried off to her post.

Jane spoke to busker after busker, turning them away, one after another, in monotonous succession. Half an hour passed, an hour passed, and still they came, singing "Lord Thomas and fair Annet, sat all day on a hill," but none possessed a blue cloak.

Discouraged, she walked to the window while awaiting the arrival of still another prospect. The fog, she saw, had thinned as had the throng though there still must have been thirty men crowding about the entrance to the house. She drew in her breath when, near the rear of the jostling throng, she caught sight of a patch of blue.

Hastening to the door, she called, "Travis!" When

the butler came to her, she said, "The man in blue, you must bring him inside."

A few minutes later Travis ushered the busker into the drawing room where he stood glancing uncertainly about him. An older man, this busker wore a blue velvet cloak that looked to be much older than he was. The King's Cloak, Jane was certain.

"How did you come by your cloak?" Jane asked.

"I come by it proper like," he said, clutching the cloak to him, "I swear I did. A man of the cloth give it to me in Spitalfields."

Elated, Jane wanted to laugh, she wanted to weep. Murmuring, "Pray wait here," she ran to the music room. "Charlotte, Charlotte," she cried, "come at once, we have the busker, we have the cloak."

When they returned to the drawing room, the busker eyed them apprehensively as he edged toward the window as though considering flight.

"Calm yourself, my good man," Charlotte told him, "we intend you no harm."

"I come by the cloak proper like," the busker said.

"We are aware that you did," Charlotte said. "The cloak was given to you by the Reverend Richard Miles in the vicinity of Brick and Church Streets. He gave it to you in error but he nonetheless gave it to you. The cloak is rightfully yours, we both realize that."

"Like I said." The busker nodded, relaxing but still warily glancing from one to the other.

"This blue cloak of yours," Charlotte went on, "may

be valuable or it may have little or no value at all. Do
you understand?"

The busker nodded doubtfully.

"We are prepared to offer you an amazingly generous sum for the cloak," Charlotte told him. "You are,
of course, free to accept or to refuse our offer."

" 'Tis a good cloak." The busker glanced down at
the blue velvet garment falling to below his knees. "A
right swaggering sort of cloak. Wearing it makes a man
feel like a king, it does."

"We will give you one hundred guineas for the
cloak," Charlotte said. "No more and no less, we shall
not haggle. You may accept or refuse, the choice is
yours."

Two hours later, Devlin arrived at Old Burlington
Street with Tommy Boggs in tow. After stepping down
from his carriage he glanced around uncertainly, surprised by the litter, mainly old newspapers, on the
street in front of his aunt's house.

Shaking his head, he started up the steps, stopping
stock-still when he heard whistling coming from above
him. "By God," he murmured to himself, "can that be
'Lord Thomas and Fair Annet' I hear?" He looked up
to see the whistler, a fair-haired young man, standing
in the open doorway.

"Alas and alack," the young whistler told him, "but
I must inform you that you have arrived too late. The
vacancy has been filled."

"The vacancy?" Devlin repeated, wondering what in the devil was going on.

"Not only has the vacancy been filled," the whistler advised as he walked slowly down the steps past Devlin, "but you would have had no chance to fill it since I observe that you do not have a blue velvet cloak."

"A blue velvet cloak?" The King's Cloak? he wondered.

"However," the whistler said, "if you make inquiries at the door, you will probably receive a quid for your trouble just as I did." Resuming his whistling, he disappeared into the thinning fog.

Devlin stared after him, shaking his head. Turning, he entered the house without ringing, Tommy following at his heels. He found Charlotte reading in the drawing room. "What is all this about a blue cloak?" he demanded. "And a quid for my trouble."

His aunt looked up from her book and smiled sweetly. "The blue cloak is the King's Cloak which, you will be pleased to learn, Jane was fortunate enough to recover several hours ago. You will not, however, receive a quid for your trouble since I know for a fact you are not a busker." Glancing behind Devlin, she raised her eyebrows. "Who is your young friend?"

Devlin ignored her question, staring at her in disbelief. "You actually found the cloak, the King's Cloak?" he asked.

"We did."

"Where is it?"

"With Jane, of course. I believe you do realize that the cloak is hers."

Devlin held on to his patience with some difficulty. "And where might Jane be found?" he asked.

"Miss Sterling has long since departed for Lyon Hall. With the cloak."

Ten

As soon as his carriage left London on its journey to the south, Devlin leaned his head back against the leather seat and closed his eyes as he tried to determine what his strategy would be after his arrival in Sussex. He was on his way not to Lyon Hall but to Fair Oaks, Lord Lansdowne's estate. Lansdowne would be surprised to see him—Devlin scarcely knew the distinguished though rather eccentric gentleman—but a mention of Ackroyd's name and a discreet hint of the Prince Regent's interest in the outcome of his quest would surely assure him a welcome. Lansdowne had been the obvious choice since Fair Oaks, the site of the famous Lansdowne Folly, was situated only a few miles to the north of Lyon Hall.

His main problem, Devlin realized, was not establishing his base of operations but rather how he could obtain the King's Cloak without revealing its secret to Jane. No doubt she would hide the cloak as soon as she reached Lyon Hall. He fully expected that when he made his appearance on the scene she would demand to know his reason for seeking the cloak. What was he to tell her? He could never reveal the truth.

Though perhaps never was too strong a word. Actually, if no other alternative presented itself, he might be forced to tell her.

He knew that he must change his tactics if he was to gain possession of the cloak. In the beginning he had expected its recovery to be a simple matter but Jane—or else fate—had forestalled him at every turn. Despite himself, he smiled, grudgingly admiring her determination and her cleverness.

Jane. He murmured her name, smiling as he pictured her in her many moods ranging from elation to despair to anger. How enchanting she looked and behaved in each of them. And when he held her in his arms, when he kissed her—he shook his head. Such intriguing images of making love to Jane led only to frustration, not to the cloak. The elusive cloak.

He had only been repulsed in his quest for the cloak, he reminded himself, he had not been defeated. He was determined to succeed and he would succeed. He was, by God, Lord Devlin, and the word failure was not to be found in the Devlin vocabulary.

The time for niceties had long since passed. He would allow nothing to stop him from finding out where Jane had concealed the cloak, he would seize it and, if indeed it was the true King's Cloak, he would recover the missing portion of the coded message left by Merriweather a century and a half ago during his flight across Southern England to France. Unfortunately, Lyon Hall offered Jane a variety of hiding places either in the main house, in one of the many outbuildings or on the extensive grounds. Despite the cloak's bulk, she could and undoubtedly would find a place of concealment, a clever one, being Jane.

There must be a way, Devlin assured himself, to discover that hiding place and recover the cloak. Jane would, of course, be on her guard and his cause had not been helped in the least by the news of the recent burning of the city of Washington by British troops. The more difficult the task, however and the higher the odds against him, the greater his satisfaction would be in finally attaining his goal.

Hearing Cunningham's voice over the pounding of the horses' hooves and the rattle of the carriage, Devlin opened his eyes and looked about him at a country vista of brown fields and hedgerows. Inexplicably, the carriage slowed, then stopped altogether. He heard his coachman clamber down from his perch, the door opened and Cunningham looked first at him and then overhead at the carriage roof.

"What the devil is it?" Devlin demanded.

"A devil, devil, right enough," Cunningham said indignantly. "That lad, he stowed aboard and now here he is as big as life."

Devlin climbed down from the carriage to the dirt roadway where he stood with hands on hips looking up at the roof, frowning when he saw Tommy Boggs lying on his stomach, both hands gripping the rail, staring back at him from wide frightened eyes.

"Get down from there," Devlin ordered.

Tommy scrinched his eyes but failed to move.

"Get down, I say," Devlin roared.

Tommy scrambled to his feet, swung himself over

the rail, and dropped to the road a few feet from Devlin. The boy stood with his hands clasped in front of him and his gaze fixed on the ground.

"Must of caught hold to the rear when we left Old Burlington," Cunningham said, "and climbed on top once we was through the toll gate."

Devlin nodded. "Explain yourself," he said to Tommy.

The boy looked up at him, almost defiantly. "You said anywhere a-tall. I heard you. Drive you anywhere you please, you said. Promised me, you did."

Devlin recollected telling the boy something of the sort. "What I might have said and what I really meant were not the same. As you, Tommy Boggs, are bright enough to know." Devlin sighed and shook his head. He was encountering one frustration after another on this ill-fated journey; now he would have to make arrangements to send the boy back to town by mail coach.

"I got nowhere to go," Tommy said desperately, his defiance faltering. Again he looked down at the ground but not before Devlin thought he espied a tear in the corner of his eye.

Despite himself, Devlin's heart went out to the boy. Tommy was, after all, an orphan just as Jane Sterling was an orphan. If Tommy were telling the truth, he had nowhere to go just as Jane would have nowhere to go when she lost Lyon Hall. If Jane were here with him now she would, he was confident, do whatever she could to help Tommy. Just as she would expect him, Devlin, to help as well.

Devlin drew in a quick breath, then smiled. What a

happy inspiration! He could be of assistance to every-body in one fell swoop, he could help Tommy, please Jane at least temporarily, and, most important, further his own cause. A wise man, he reminded himself, makes use of whatever happens to come to hand.

"Are you absolutely certain you have no home," he asked the boy, "no people anywhere, no one waiting for your return, expecting you, perhaps at this very moment preparing to go in search of you?"

"No one," Tommy said. "I swear on the Bible, no one."

Again Devlin was struck by the boy's manner. Wher-ever the lad might have come from, he was not the common type of arab found wandering about the city. "If I allow you to come with me," he said, "and find you a place where you can earn your keep, perhaps learn a useful trade by becoming an apprentice, if I do that will you in return do a few small favors for me?"

Tommy nodded eagerly.

"Capital," Devlin said with a satisfied smile. "We shall help one another. Now climb up into the carriage so I may be on my way to Fair Oaks. I have great plans for you, Tommy Boggs. Do you know what you shall be?"

Tommy shook his head.

"You shall be my Trojan horse."

Following breakfast on the day after she arrived back at Lyon Hall, Jane climbed to the attic in the west wing with Chatter following close behind. Her purpose, or so she told herself, was to search for a place to hide the cloak she had recovered from the busker. Devlin, she vowed, would not lay hands on the cloak, her cloak, until he revealed his reason for so avidly seeking it.

Upon returning to Lyon Hall the night before she had carried the cloak to her bed chamber—where it was at this very moment—and carefully picked open one side of the lining. When she found nothing hidden between the lining and the outer cloth she wondered for a moment if this was the authentic King's Cloak. She quickly dismissed her doubts for Charlotte had been certain that the tailor's label—"Cavendish"— dated from the seventeenth century.

After a cursory search for hiding places in the attic, Jane walked to the window to look along the avenue leading to the Midhurst Road. Devlin must have followed her to Lyon Hall, he would never give up easily. But he had not arrived the night before and, to her intense disappointment, there was no sign of him yet. She lingered at the window with Chatter curling himself about her feet, her gaze on the road, admitting to herself that this was the real reason she had come to the attic.

Was it possible Devlin had been telling her the truth all along? Could he have been interested in finding the cloak only to aid her, to help her save Lyon Hall from the money lenders? Now that she had retrieved the cloak without Devlin's assistance and made a hasty departure from London without so much as saying goodbye, might he have decided she was not worth helping and turned his back on her?

Jane felt a heartbreaking pang of loss as she realized she might never see him again.

What was that? Her pulses raced as a curricle with a matched pair of greys drove from under the trees onto the sweep of the drive. Yes, yes, it was Devlin, reins in hand. But who sat beside him? It looked like a boy wearing an oversized and ragged coat. How very odd.

Jane hurried from the attic and was halfway down the stairs to the ground floor when, hearing Devlin's voice coming from the drawing room, she stopped of a sudden. It would never do to appear too eager, to come into his presence so obviously out of breath. She must calm her foolish heart, must be friendly to Devlin but aloof, be gracious but not overly warm.

Seeing Estelle leave the drawing room, Jane walked slowly down the stairs to meet her.

"I was on my way to your room to fetch you," Estelle said, "for I do believe that Lord Devlin desires to speak with you in private concerning a confidential matter." She glanced behind her and sighed. "He is certainly a most elegant gentleman."

As Jane neared the drawing room, she smoothed her hair, wishing she had taken the time to glance at herself in a glass. Considering the dust in the attic it was even possible she might have a smudge on her nose.

When she entered, Devlin sprang to his feet and crossed the room to meet her, raising her hand to his lips, making her forget her worry over her appearance.

Yes, she thought, he *was* elegant in his forest green waistcoat, green and black checked trousers and his grey cravat. In his case the man made the clothes, not the other way around.

"You probably suspect I came for the King's Cloak," he said, motioning toward the King's Room where the false cloak remained on display.

Her elation at seeing him faded. The King's Cloak, always the King's Cloak, she thought bitterly. Controlling her annoyance, she said nothing.

"Such, however, is not the case," he went on, "since I have returned to Sussex not for the cloak—ah, I see that does surprise you!—but to stay for a few days with Lord Lansdowne at Fair Oaks, the gentleman I was on my way to visit when, through misadventure, I first came to Lyon Hall."

"The cloak no longer interests you?" Disbelief threaded through her voice.

"My only object in pursuing the cloak so single-mindedly was to help you, Jane, by finding out if the cloak was authentic. Alas, I failed to win your trust, you showed that by hastily leaving London with the cloak, so I have decided to wash my hands of the whole affair."

Should she believe him? Jane wondered. His sudden indifference to the cloak aroused her suspicions and also, for reasons she could not define, disappointed her more than she cared to admit.

"I came to Lyon Hall today not for the cloak nor merely to retrieve Horatio from your stableboy—Joshua?—but to put myself in your debt by begging a favor." Devlin stepped aside and gestured behind him.

Jane, her attention drawn from Devlin for the first time since entering the room, became aware of a thin redheaded boy who had been standing behind Devlin— hiding behind him might be more accurate because now that he had been revealed to her the boy would not meet her gaze.

"This," Devlin said, "is Master Tommy Boggs, a London orphan, a boy with nowhere in the world to call home. He came to my assistance yesterday in town and, after I befriended him, he became, all unbe- knownst to myself, a passenger on top of my carriage when I left for Sussex."

At the sound of his name, Jane noticed, Tommy had ducked his head even lower so that he seemed to be staring at his scuffed, ill-fitting shoes. Although his face and hair looked newly scrubbed, his cheeks had an unhealthy pallor. How small he seemed, how alone and defenseless, how terribly in need of someone to care for him.

"I hesitate to impose the lad on old Lansdowne," Devlin said. "Could you possibly find a place for him here at Lyon Hall until I return to town? I shall take him with me when I leave Fair Oaks for London and have promised to find a suitable place for him there. I should be leaving in a week or so."

Jane walked to Tommy. "Would you please look at me?" she asked. When he raised cautious brown eyes to meet her gaze, she smiled. "Would you like to stay here with me for a while? My Aunt Estelle and I would love to have you."

As Tommy once again ducked his head, Jane realized that, though she spoke the truth, at the same time she realized she had another, hidden motive in offering shelter to young Tommy Boggs. Keeping the boy at Lyon Hall would give her a tie to Devlin.

Looking everywhere but at Jane, Tommy glanced at Devlin before shyly nodding his head.

"Then you shall be our guest," Jane said.

"Guest," Tommy whispered so faintly she wasn't sure she had heard him correctly.

"Excellent!" Devlin brought his hands together with a resounding clap. "That, then, is settled. Tommy and I thank you exceedingly." He started to go on only to hesitate and then bow to her in farewell. He seemed torn between a desire to linger and a determination to leave now that his business had been accomplished.

Jane watched him, saying nothing, wanting him to stay but unwilling to tell him directly or even offer him an excuse to help him delay his departure.

"Have you seen the Lansdowne Folly?" Devlin asked.

Jane shook her head. "I wanted to ride there soon after I came to Lyon Hall but was informed that Lord Lansdowne discouraged visitors."

"He does indeed and yet he leaves his Folly untouched when he could easily have had all traces of it removed, seeming to be of two minds, ashamed of what happened to his grand scheme while at the same

time proud of his achievement." His gaze captured
hers. "Will you ride with me to the Folly tomorrow?"

She tried to suppress her eagerness and failed. "Oh,
yes," she said, "that would be lovely."

"Early," Devlin said, suddenly becoming awkward.
"Early in the morning. I shall call for you at ten."
Again he bowed. "Until tomorrow. Until the Folly."

"The Folly," she echoed softly as she watched him
leave.

M. Claude LaSalle called on Jane that same afternoon.

"I am here, Mlle. Sterling," the debonair Frenchman
said after they were seated in the drawing room, "to
extend an invitation to a ball to be held at my residence, Montcalm House." He reached inside his waistcoat and, with a flourish, handed her a sealed envelope.
"The others, and I am inviting absolutely everyone in
this part of Sussex, will receive their invitations by the
post. Yours, I bring in person to assure myself of your
acceptance."

As Jane broke the seal and scanned the hand-written
invitation, LaSalle leaned over and stroked Chatter's
fur. The ball, Jane saw, would be held at Montcalm
House on the following Saturday evening.

"I regret exceedingly," M. LaSalle said in his ac-
cented English, "the briefness of the notice but my
inspiration arrived with an unexpected velocity only
two days ago following our meeting while on horse-

back. You will attend, will you not, mademoiselle? And your companion, Miss Estelle Winward, as well?"

Jane hesitated briefly, aware she had nothing suitable to wear to a ball. Then she thought of the attics with their wardrobes and trunks crammed with outmoded gowns. Maud might well be able to refashion one for her and, perhaps, another for Estelle.

"We shall both be delighted to come," she told him, smiling.

"How happy you make me, Mlle. Sterling. My entertainment is thus assured of being a success even if no one else makes an appearance. The English, you understand, may not yet be prepared to accept the hospitality of a former enemy."

"The English have been flocking to Paris since the peace," she said, "and so I feel certain they will come to Montcalm House. Your ball will be a great success whether I attend or not."

"Not at all, not at all, your presence is essential, at least to me. When first I met you I said to myself, 'Claude, this Jane Sterling, this young lady from America, is a most extraordinary person.' After living all forty years of my life in France, mostly in Paris, I must confide in you that I find the ladies of England rather dull and dowdy. But you, Mlle. Sterling, have more French *panache,* more high spirits, than any mademoiselle ever possessed."

His extravagant compliments warmed her, no matter how insincere she suspected them to be. "You exaggerate," she protested. "Besides, I myself am English, or at least most of my ancestors were."

"Ah, the Lyon family, famous, or so I am told, for the beauty of their women and the improvidence of their men. The women married wealth and the men proceeded to squander it. And also renowned for possessing the King's Cloak. At least I believe you told me you have such a garment here at Lyon Hall."

Jane sighed inwardly. Was M. LaSalle, like Devlin, interested in the King's Cloak to the exclusion of all else? Was his invitation and his flattery merely ploys to discover more about the cloak? She nodded toward the open door to the King's Room.

"But yes," M. LaSalle said, "I see the cloak in all its glory." He looked at Jane and smiled. "I regret that your famous cloak fails to excite my curiosity," he said. "When conversing with a charming woman, a ragged piece of English cloth, no matter how ancient, holds no allure whatsoever for Claude LaSalle."

She wondered whether she should tell the Frenchman that the cloak in the glass case was only a copy of the original. No, she decided, there was no reason to take him into her confidence.

"I often wonder," she said, thinking of Devlin and his scheme to make off with the cloak, "if I should take special precautions to protect the cloak. I sometimes wonder whether there might be those unscrupulous enough to steal it. I refer to Englishmen," she hastened to add, "not Frenchmen."

"*My* scruples are of the best," M. LaSalle assured her. "A charming woman such as yourself might tempt me to commit an indiscretion; a blue cloak, no matter how valuable, never would. Many Englishmen, being a rather peculiar breed, might prefer the cloak."

"At least some Englishmen would," Jane said, again recalling Devlin's avid pursuit of the cloak. She blinked, all at once thinking of the perfect place to hide the cloak, a place where no one, Devlin in particular, would ever consider looking. Or would they? Devlin did possess a devious mind.

"You and I," M. LaSalle was saying, "should become the best of friends for we have so very much in common. My country, especially the General Lafayette, helped America in its war of independence against the British tyrants and now once more America and France stand shoulder to shoulder."

"But Napoleon is on Elba; France has lost the war."

"It is true, Napoleon is in exile at the moment." LaSalle rose and walked to the fireplace. "But Elba is not far distant from France. If he returns from exile, if he escapes his prison, and I do believe he will, and soon, my countrymen will take up arms once more. Not, of course, against America."

"And you, M. LaSalle, what will you do if Napoleon returns to France?"

LaSalle paced back and forth, his eyes sparkling with fervor, his hands gesticulating as he spoke. "I shall join him, of a certainty I shall join him, as will all loyal Frenchmen. Napoleon will fight for the glory of France, he will carry the banner of the revolution throughout all of Europe, he will spread our great ideal of 'Liberty, Equality, and Fraternity' to all the world. England is old and slowly dying while France is young and vibrant. England is the past, France is the future, a future I hope to help shape on the anvil of history."

Jane, taken aback by the Frenchman's zeal, stared at him. "Do you think so little of the Bourbons then?" she asked.

"Paugh! The English king is mad but the Bourbons are worse than mad, they are fools." LaSalle stopped pacing and came to sit beside Jane on the settee. "As I am," he said, leaning toward her.

"Surely not, M. LaSalle. Your enthusiasm does you credit."

"But I am a fool nonetheless. Here I am enjoying a *tête-à-tête* with the enchanting Mlle. Sterling and how do I conduct myself? Do I compliment her on her wit? But no. Do I admire her marvelous auburn hair, her exquisite face, her flashing hazel eyes? I do not. Rather I squander these precious moments discussing the politics. Will you ever see fit to pardon me?"

"Of course," she said, blushing a little at his effusive compliments.

"And you *will* attend the ball at Montcalm House? You must come without fail."

"How could I possibly refuse such a warm and heartfelt invitation? I shall be there as, I am certain, will Miss Winward."

Standing, M. LaSalle raised Jane's hand to his lips. "I bid you not goodbye," he said, "rather *au revoir*— until we meet again. As we shall, and soon."

* * *

Jane watched from the drawing room window as M. LaSalle rode away on a spirited black horse, the silver ornaments on saddle and bridle glittering in the sun. Tommy Boggs, she noted absently, who stood next to a yew across the drive, was watching the Frenchman, too.

She shook her head, frowning. Not over Tommy—naturally he would be fascinated by so colorful a figure. No, it was her own feelings that puzzled her. Unlike Devlin on his first visit to Lyon Hall, M. LaSalle had shown little or no interest in the King's Cloak; he professed to be interested only in her. Although she found his praise excessive, she was certain he genuinely wanted her to attend the ball since his insistence had the ring of truth. She wanted to go since not only did she love music and dancing, she looked forward to meeting her Sussex neighbors during an evening of bright, swirling excitement.

Why then, she asked herself, did her thoughts return again and again not to the ball but to tomorrow morning's promised ride with Devlin to the Lansdowne Folly?

Eleven

Early the next morning Jane took the King's Cloak from her bed chamber and carried the heavy blue garment to its new place of concealment. Dusting her hands together, she smiled in satisfaction. No one could possibly find it now, not even Devlin. Of course he had denied further interest in the cloak; she did not, however, believe him, not crediting his tale of returning to Sussex merely to visit Lord Lansdowne. When he first arrived at Lyon Hall, Devlin had never mentioned Lansdowne. She wondered if the visit had been arranged only after she stole a march on him in Town by recovering the cloak.

Her suspicions of his motives did not, however, prevent a leap of her heart when Devlin arrived at the Hall promptly at ten. By then the morning mist had risen and, as they rode east, she relished the unusual warmth of the November day, a brief surcease from the chill and damp of the approaching winter. The fog blanketing London, she supposed, had heralded this change in the weather.

As they cantered along a lane, Jane could not help but be aware of Devlin's many appreciative glances.

Was he showing his approval because today she rode sidesaddle to please his English sense of propriety? Or could it be her riding costume, Maud's spur-of-the-moment creation, a light blue gown worn with a darker blue spencer, both gown and spencer featuring a lower cut bodice than she was accustomed to wearing.

Despite Maud's insistence that, " 'Tis modest, miss, compared to some," Jane had felt a bit uneasy about her décolletage. Devlin's obvious admiration, though, lent her assurance. Perhaps she should try to be more modish, not so much for Devlin as for her own sake. *He* was not to be trusted, though he did have a good heart as his effort to help Tommy Boggs proved.

"Tommy is a bright lad," Jane said as they left the lane and rode beside an overgrown hedgerow of holly and rosebushes. "He can even read and write, not well but more than what one would expect. He must have had at least a smattering of schooling."

Devlin scowled. "He may read and write," he said, "but he also happens to be a thief, born and bred."

Taken aback—she had assumed Devlin felt a fondness for the lad—she felt compelled to protest. "Bred perhaps, but surely not born. Babies are innocents; a boy has to be taught to be dishonest. Besides, what makes you so certain he *is* a thief?"

Devlin shrugged. "It's of no real consequence. Nevertheless, I warn you to beware of giving your heart to the lad. I fear Tommy Boggs is the kind who offers his loyalty to the man or woman offering him the greatest reward."

Jane gave Devlin a hard look but made no reply.

How cynical he sounded this morning! Today he seemed so very different from the Devlin who had confided his secret dreams to her at the Angel Inn. What could have happened to change him in such a short time?

They rode in silence for nearly a mile. "I always thought," Devlin said at last, slowing his horse's pace, "that I believed in a code of chivalry."

When he paused, Jane stared at him, wondering what had brought chivalry to his mind and why he seemed to be having difficulty expressing himself.

"One of my fellow officers on the Peninsula," Devlin went on, "maintained that a gentleman must ride straight, speak the truth, and never show fear. He believed the tests of a gentleman were the keeping of one's word and the offering of succor to the helpless. The true measure of civilization, he maintained, was how the men treated the women. And at the time, I agreed with him."

"And now you have doubts of some sort?" she asked.

"I discovered that being chivalrous in this imperfect world of ours was easier said than done. There comes a time when a man is faced with a choice and whatever he may choose is both right and wrong. What he does may help someone while at the same time injuring another. So he makes his choice as best he can and goes on with his life even though he leaves hurt and bitterness behind him."

Was he speaking of something he had done recently? Jane wondered. "I know of no one who feels bitterness toward you," she said, "so perhaps I do not fully understand your concern."

Devlin slowed his horse's pace further and they rode side by side at a walk. He reached to her and, after a brief hesitation, she offered him her hand. "Whatever happens," he said, "remember that I did what I thought was right." Releasing her hand, he spurred his horse ahead.

Puzzled, she urged her horse on, overtaking him as the path they followed zigzagged back and forth to climb a low hill. "Is it the cloak?" she asked.

He smiled ruefully. "You seem to believe all of my waking moments are spent contriving ways to regain the King's Cloak. You probably imagine my dreams are filled with visions of the cloak."

"At times it seems that way," she acknowledged.

Devlin raised his arm as a king giving a command might. "I hereby order the King's Cloak to be banished from our minds," he said, "for at least the remainder of this day. Do you agree to abide by my decree?"

"I do, my lord," she said.

"Excellent." He nodded above them to the bare crest of the hill. "We shall have our first view of the Folly from the summit," he told her.

Jane nodded and, as the path narrowed, she guided her gelding behind his up toward the top of the hill. This ride with Devlin to the Folly, so avidly anticipated, was somehow threatening to turn sour. She searched her memory to try to decide where the change had begun. Tommy, Tommy Boggs? Her casual mention of the boy seemed to have started the wrongness. She had no notion why.

When Devlin reined in, she rode up to stop beside him. He smiled at her. "How enchanting you look," he said. "Not your riding costume, Jane, though it does become you, but you yourself."

His few words of admiration meant more to her than all the lavish praises of Claude LaSalle ever could. At the same time she wondered if he, too, had sensed something awry between them and was trying to change the downward spiral of the day.

"There you have the Lansdowne Folly," Devlin said.

Putting her worrisome thoughts aside, determined to recapture the bright promise of the day, she gazed down at the meadow below them where the gigantic, tilting base of a stone tower rose twenty feet into the air, ending in a jagged circular top. To the right of the tower, clusters of huge smooth-sided stones lay scattered across the meadow for a distance of more than a hundred feet.

"When he came into his inheritance," Devlin said, "Lord Lansdowne decided to erect the tallest building in all of England and name it the Lansdowne Tower. He hired a famous architect, George Grambling, and had the stones carted here all the way from Wales. Alas, when the tower reached a height of one hundred and fifty feet, the right side of the base began to sink into the ground and the tower began to tilt; nothing Grambling could do slowed the process and eventually the tower collapsed much like the Tower of Babel must have done. That was thirty years ago; the Lansdowne

Tower became known as the Lansdowne Folly and
Lord Lansdowne went into seclusion."

"There must be a moral to such a sad story," Jane
said.

"The Bible gives us one: 'Pride goeth before de-
struction, and an haughty spirit before a fall.' "

"Exactly so. But I still feel sorry for Lord Lansdowne. Proud though he might have been, he harmed
himself most of all. As proud men are wont to do."

Devlin shot her a quick glance before reining his
horse toward a path leading down the gradual slope.
"Follow me to the ruins," he said.

When they reached the bottom of the hill, Jane saw
that the fallen blocks of stone were even more massive
than she had thought, rising well above her head.
Devlin led the way between the stones, turning first
one way and then another as though threading his way
through a maze. When he came to the tower's circular
base, he stopped, swung to the ground and then helped
Jane dismount before he tethered the horses.

They walked clockwise around the base until they
came to an opening in the five-foot thick wall. Inside,
fragments of stone littered the paved floor; across from
where they stood a staircase began an upward spiral
only to end abruptly. Above the broken top of the wall,
Jane saw the bright blue of the cloudless sky.

"A stairway leading nowhere," Jane murmured.

Devlin looked at her and, for a moment before turning away, she thought she saw anguish clouding his
eyes. "I should never have brought you to the Folly,"

Devlin said. "There seems to be a feeling of futility here."

"I wanted to come," Jane insisted, while finding herself unable to dispel the sense of sadness, of impending discord and unhappiness.

Devlin turned back to her, his lips curled into a smile that never reached his eyes.

"I have a surprise for you." He offered her his arm, she took it and he escorted her around the tower to the far side where, on top of one of the smaller fallen blocks of stone she saw a wicker picnic basket resting on a plaid blanket. "I left these here earlier on my way to Lyon Hall," he said.

Jane clapped her hands in delight, feeling some of the gloomy miasma vanish. "A picnic! What a marvelous idea." She noticed that her words made his smile grow warmer, more genuine.

Finding a sunny spot in the midst of the huge rocks, Devlin spread the blanket on the still-green grass. Jane opened the basket and brought forth bread and a variety of cheeses, a bottle of Madeira, two glasses, knives and napkins. They sat on the blanket facing one another and, as they ate and sipped the wine, they talked of childhood escapades, of memories of other days and other picnics, again sharing the easy intimacy they had known at the Angel Inn.

After they finished their meal, Devlin leaned forward and touched her arm lightly. "Sometimes," he said, "I wish I could journey to some remote South Sea isle or to a snowbound mountain cottage, not by myself but with one I loved, and live there in seclusion, just the two of us, far removed from the turbulence of this world."

She was transfixed, picturing the two of them sitting beneath a palm tree, hand in hand. Returning to her senses, Jane reminded herself *she* was not necessarily the one Devlin had meant. Since he was gazing at her expectantly she had to answer but, unsure how to reply, she said lightly, "I believe you would soon become bored."

Devlin sighed. "Quite right," he said. "I would quickly grow weary of such a monotonous life and begin to crave the excitement of London. It was only an impractical and romantic dream." Turning from her he knelt and began repacking the picnic hamper.

Jane's heart sank. Inexplicably she felt that in some way she had failed him. Impulsively she leaned toward him, wanting to reassure him with a touch, but then she stopped, thinking better of it. Rising, she walked a short distance away, putting him beyond her reach as she reminded herself she did not know what Devlin wanted. So how could she possibly help him?

The gigantic stone blocks loomed over her, hemming her in, seeming to press on her from all sides. If only there was a vista of a stream or woods or fields or of the distant Downs, but she could see nothing except the giant grey stones. Thinking she saw an opening, she made her way along a corridor between stones, but when she came to a turning she found herself even deeper within the maze.

Trying to retrace her steps, she turned and walked back the way she believed she had come. On reaching a turning in the corridor, however, she saw not Devlin but more shadowed alleyways running between the massive debris of the fallen tower. She was gripped by an unreasoning fear.

"Devlin!" she called. The words echoed from the giant blocks of stone.

"Jane," Devlin answered a mere heartbeat later. "Where are you?"

Relieved, she walked swiftly in the direction of his voice. Again she called his name and again he answered only now he seemed farther away than before. Shaking her head in frustration, she looked up at the truncated tower and made her way in that direction, intending to circle its base until she left the wilderness of fallen stones behind.

After two wrong turns she came to the circular wall and followed it to her right, looking for the entryway where she and Devlin had paused a short time before. In a few minutes, she was sure, she would be on her way out of the maze. She walked on only to find stones blocking her way. She was in another cul-de-sac.

"Jane."

She swung around. Devlin stood at the entrance to the cul-de-sac. She wanted to run to him.

"I thought—" he began, striding toward her, his eyes dark and fathomless. "I thought I'd lost you."

He came to her, gripped her by the shoulders, pulled her to him and kissed her. Alarmed by his intensity, she instinctively drew away, trying to turn her head from his, sensing in him a desperation, an underlying hint of violence she failed to understand. His hand went to her nape, preventing her escape, and his kiss grew more passionate and demanding.

She put her hands to his chest in an effort to push him away. Suddenly he released her, his breath rasping in his throat. He stared at her, the pain in his brown eyes piercing her heart.

"Devlin?" she murmured when he stepped back.

She ached with the sense that their time together was nearing an end, that the sand in the hourglass had almost run out. They had somehow lost their way and now it was too late to turn back and start anew. She had no choice, she must seize whatever this moment offered for there would be no second chance.

"Devlin," she repeated, a catch in her voice as she reached to him.

He took her in his arms, enfolding her, kissing her, his lips possessing hers, a breathtaking kiss. She put her arms around him, holding him to her, moaning as if in pain as she surrendered herself to him. For now. For ever. Devlin, Devlin, Devlin.

After a time of heartstopping wonder, he again stepped away from her, looking as dazed as she felt. He slowly shook his head. She thought she heard him murmur, "God."

He seized her hand and, turning on his heel, he strode away, pulling her with him, his pace so fast she had to run to keep up. They came to the tethered horses and he put his hands to her waist to lift her into the saddle, then he paused, looking into her eyes, his face enigmatic. She drew in her breath, waiting, expectant, but then he lifted her onto her mount, released her and, without a word, swung onto his own horse.

They rode back to Lyon Hall, saying little. He left her at the stable, his hand touching hers briefly but with only a mumbled word of parting, and rode away, her gaze following him until he entered the woods and was gone.

Jane walked slowly into the garden and sat on a bench beneath an arbor where the uncut stalks of the flowers spoke of a lack of care. She had been shaken by Devlin's passionate embrace, unsettled by her own ardent response. At the same time she gloried in the knowledge that she could evoke such emotion in him.

Yet she was disturbed by the unexpected edge of violence in Devlin, a violence that both repelled and attracted her. Something was wrong, terribly wrong, perhaps only with Devlin, perhaps between Devlin and herself. Her thoughts were in a turmoil; she found it difficult to think sensibly but realized she must. If only she could discover what had caused Devlin's strange behavior.

The true trouble, she knew, centered on the cloak and, more recently, in some way on young Tommy Boggs. Devlin had befriended the boy in London, brought him to Sussex with him, promising to find a place for him on his return to town. Why then did he insist on branding him a thief? She would speak to Tommy, Jane decided, and try to find out more about the boy, see if she could determine what Tommy wanted for himself, not what Devlin might want for him. She might not be able to help herself or Devlin but perhaps she could help Tommy Boggs.

Leaving the garden, she returned to the house where she found Estelle having lunch in the morning room. "Tommy?" Estelle said in reply to Jane's question. "I saw Tommy earlier in the drawing room. Or was he in the King's Room? One or the other. And I saw him later down near the stables. That boy seems to be everywhere and yet nowhere."

That was the way boys were, Jane knew, remembering the three Pariot brothers. She rang for Hendricks.

"Master Boggs?" Hendricks frowned in thought. "The lad was helping Mrs. Archer peel potatoes in the kitchen early on. Then I spied him near the spring house but when I looked a moment later he was gone."

"Please have Alice see if he went back to his room," Jane told Hendricks.

Tommy was not in his room nor was he in the attic, nor in the servants' quarters nor in either of the wings. He must, Jane decided, have gone on a ramble to explore the grounds. Intending to talk to the boy when he returned, she went to the book room, intending to learn as much as she could about the reigns of Charles I and Charles II, hoping their histories might contain a clue to the secret of the King's Cloak.

She was reaching for a book on one of the higher shelves on the library's far wall when she heard what sounded like an intake of breath behind her. Turning, she found Tommy staring at her from where he sat in a massive armchair, a book open on his lap. When she had glanced into the library earlier she had failed to see him.

"Are you reading?" she asked.

Tommy shook his head, guiltily, Jane thought. "Looking at the pictures," he said. The book on his lap, she saw, contained drawings of horses and carriages.

Sitting on a stool at the foot of the bookcase, Jane asked, "Would you like to work with horses? Be a post boy, perhaps? Or a coachman after you grow up?"

Tommy shook his head.

"What would you like to be?" she persisted, determined to help him in spite of himself.

Tommy shrugged.

"Your father," Jane said, wondering if Tommy had any memory at all of his parents. "What trade did your father follow?"

Tommy stared down at the book on his lap and for a long time she thought he would not answer her but then he said, "He was a—a—" He frowned as though searching his memory for the right word. "An artist," he said at last. "My father was an artist."

"He painted?" she asked in surprise.

"There was paintings everywhere." Tommy swung his arm to include the entire room, becoming animated as he talked. "Paintings hanging on the walls, stacked on the floor, in all the rooms, I was always falling over a painting of his." The light left his eyes and once again he stared down at the book. "And then he died," he said dully, "and they come and took the paintings away and then they come and took me away."

Jane went to him, took his hand and squeezed it tightly. "No one will take you away from anywhere again," she promised. "Not if you want to stay."

When Tommy made no response, she walked to the desk and brought him a sheet of paper and a pencil. "Do you draw?" she asked.

He shook his head.

"Would you like to try?" she asked. When he failed to say either yea or nay, she said, "Draw a picture for me, Tommy. Please."

Placing the paper on the open book, he hunched over, the pencil moving rapidly back and forth. After a few minutes he pushed the paper away. Jane took it and saw he had drawn a galloping horse. Although the drawing was rough and unskilled, Tommy had somehow managed to convey the exciting sense of the horse's grace and speed.

"Why, you draw very well," Jane told him, "much better than I do." Was there any possible future for the boy as an artist? she wondered.

"Is that a Trojan horse?" Tommy asked.

She stared at him, wondering if she had heard right. "No," she told him. "A Trojan horse would never gallop. Do you really mean a Trojan horse?"

Tommy nodded. "A Trojan horse," he insisted.

"Do you have any notion what a Trojan horse is?"

Tommy shook his head.

Handing him back the picture, she again sat on the stool. "Troy was an ancient city in Asia," she told him. "When Greece and Troy went to war, the Greeks sailed to Troy, laid siege to the city but were unable to either scale the walls or batter them down. So they pretended to give up the siege and sailed away, leaving an enormous wooden horse behind. The Trojans opened their gates and dragged the horse inside their walls and that night the Greek soldiers who were hiding inside came out and defeated the Trojans."

She noticed that Tommy was staring at her, enraptured. "So when someone mentions a Trojan horse," she said, "they mean something underhanded or someone that tries to conquer by means of lies or trickery. Do you understand?"

Tommy's gaze left hers as he nodded. Suddenly he closed the book and sent it thudding to the floor. Leaping to his feet, he backed away from her and then turned and fled from the room, leaving Jane staring after him.

What could have upset him so? she wondered. It must be something to do with the horse, the Trojan horse. Where on earth could he have heard that expression? From his father, the artist? Highly unlikely since that had been so long ago. But who else would say those words in Tommy's presence? Could it have been Devlin? Even so, she failed to understand why Tommy would be so disturbed on learning the meaning of the phrase.

Her breath caught. Was Tommy himself the Trojan horse? Was it possible Devlin had left Tommy at Lyon Hall to serve some purpose of Devlin's and now she had made the boy realize the deviousness of his role? Because Devlin's purpose could only be to recover the King's Cloak. Jane nodded, convinced Devlin was try-

ing to deceive her once more, this time by using poor
Tommy. This would explain Tommy seeming to be
here, there and everywhere around Lyon Hall. He was
searching for the cloak. For Devlin.

There was no end to Devlin's lies, to his treachery.
This time he had gone too far, much too far. Clenching
her hands into fists, she vowed that she would find a
way to give him a much deserved comeuppance. Just
as the Folly had fallen, so would Devlin and she would
applaud his downfall with the greatest satisfaction.

Twelve

After Jane drew on her pink gloves and smoothed them over her hands and forearms, she sat in front of her dressing table looking glass while Maud carefully placed a coronet of pale pink silk rosebuds intertwined with green leaves on her auburn hair.

Standing, she crossed the room to the pier glass, smiling with surprised delight as she admired the high-waisted white chiffon gown with its frilled edges, the frills not only at the hem but also on the short, puffed sleeves, and at the rather daringly low, square neckline.

"Maud," she exclaimed, "you have worked a double miracle. This gown is not only the height of fashion but also the most becoming dress I ever wore."

Maud, a comely, dark-haired girl, blushed happily. "Had a time, I did, with those appliques," she said, nodding at the bands of pink crossed over Jane's bodice and, above the hem, the applique of entwined green leaves between two more bands of pink. "But I can see 'twas worth the work."

"An exquisite touch," Jane said, turning and hugging Maud. "How can I ever thank you?"

" 'Tis me should be thanking you, miss, for giving

me a place to live here at Lyon Hall, considering. Not many would've taken me in what with me being in the family way and all."

Maud and I are alike in one way, Jane thought, both of us have been deceived by men. Maud's sailor lover had deceived her while Devlin, in a very different way, deceived me.

"Without you, Maud," she said, "I could never be on my way to M. LaSalle's ball tonight. You have truly been my fairy godmother."

She might go to the ball, she reminded herself ruefully, but, alas, no prince awaited her at Montcalm House.

As Jane started to leave the bed chamber, Maud said, "Wait, you don't want to forget this." The seamstress gathered a white silk shawl, its edges embroidered with green leaves and pink flowers, from the bed and draped it over Jane's shoulders. "Pretty as any picture, you are," she said. " 'Tisn't only the gown, miss, 'tis you, yourself, as well."

Jane smiled at Maud, then, aware that Estelle must be waiting in the drawing room, hastened down the stairs, the toes of her pink slippers visible under the hem of her gown. She had never felt quite so fashionable.

"Pray give me a moment," she said to Estelle as she hurried past into the King's Room.

Wishing to be absolutely certain that the cloak was still where she had hidden it after her return from London, Jane opened the glass case, lifting the edge of the blue cloak to read the label: "Cavendish." She nod-

ded in satisfaction. Just so, the King's Cloak was safe
in its case, masquerading as the replica of itself.

Despite all his cleverness, Devlin would never think
to look in such an obvious place, she assured herself.
Nor would Tommy Boggs if, as she suspected, the boy
had been sent to Lyon Hall to find the cloak's hiding
place and report it to Devlin. How dare Devlin use
poor Tommy in such an underhanded way!

Involving the innocent lad in his deviousness made
her all the more determined that Devlin would never
see the King's Cloak again. When Lyon Hall was sold,
she would take the cloak with her to America rather
than surrender it to him or to anyone else. She had
heard nothing from Devlin since their picnic at the
Folly which, she told herself, was just as well since
she never wanted to see Devlin again.

As she closed the case, she thought she caught a
glimpse of movement reflected in the glass of the door.
Whirling around, she looked through the open doorway
into the hall but saw no one. Hurrying into the hall,
she glanced in both directions. Still nothing; she had
probably been mistaken, Jane told herself.

"Did you see anyone in the hall while I was in the
King's Room?" she asked Estelle after they left the
house and were climbing the steps to the carriage.

"In the hall? No, no one except Chatter and I would
have because I was on the *qui vive* since I was watching for you. No doubt the cat was searching for Tommy
Boggs. He seems to have grown uncommonly attached
to the boy." Estelle smiled as they settled themselves
in the carriage for the short drive to Montcalm House.

"You look lovely, Jane," she said with genuine admiration.

Since Estelle's high-waisted tamboured mauve muslin gown was quite modish, Jane was able to honestly return the compliment.

"Ah," Estelle said, "but M. LaSalle will most certainly be smitten with you, not me."

"Whether smitten or not, and I very much doubt he will be, I shall never know for certain since I find it impossible to tell whether he truly admires me or is merely being polite. He dispenses extravagant compliments with such a lavish hand I doubt whether he has any left when he really is in need of one." M. LaSalle, she added to herself, was as false in his way as Devlin was in his. She had no interest in either gentleman, if indeed the word gentleman could be applied to either of them.

"How colorful," Estelle said as she looked from the carriage window.

The avenue leading to Montcalm House glowed with the lights from scores of Chinese lanterns hanging in the trees. Between the twin columns flanking the entrance to the house the word "PEACE" had been emblazoned above an expertly rendered painting of the hands of two women clasping above the blue waves of a sea.

"The hands," Claude LaSalle explained when he greeted them in the foyer, "are those of *La Belle* France and Britannia joined over the waters of the English Channel, signifying the new-found harmony between our two nations." In keeping with his hands-across-the-

Channel theme, Jane noted, he was dressed in the English rather than the more extravagant French mode.

This public image of M. LaSalle as an advocate of peace and harmony, she told herself, was quite different from the private LaSalle who advocated Napoleon's return to power. She was not, however, surprised to discover the Frenchman to be two-faced. After her encounters with Devlin during the last few weeks, she would, in fact, be astonished to find any man who was not.

"You must, I pray," M. LaSalle said to Jane, "grant me two requests. First, that I may have your permission to address you as Jane while you, in turn, call me Claude, the second that you honor me with the first dance of the evening."

Jane curtsied her consent.

"How gracious you are," Claude said with a smile. "I must warn you, the first dance will be rather daring, a waltz, but, I understand, waltzes are expected to be all the rage in London this season."

"I have no qualms about flouting English tradition," Jane told him.

Claude took her hand and, leaning to her, said in a low voice, "And you should have none since you, Jane, are the loveliest young lady in all of Sussex if not in all of England. Beauty must be allowed special privileges."

"You, Claude," she said, "are one of the greatest fabulists in all of Sussex if not all of England."

"A fabulist?" he repeated. "Ah," he said, smiling, "I comprehend your meaning—you believe I may embroider the truth as one does in creating a fable—but I hasten to deny your accusation." Releasing her hand, he bowed and said, "Until later."

Leaving the foyer, Jane and Estelle were drawn by the pulse of talk and laughter to the top of the marble steps above the ballroom where they found themselves looking down at a colorful mosaic of beautifully gowned ladies, their jewels sparkling in the light from the three multitiered chandeliers, escorted by attentive gentlemen garbed in the height of fashion.

The room provided M. LaSalle's guests with a perfect setting. Long and rather narrow with a gleaming parquet floor, the ballroom suggested an Italian Renaissance villa with two columns of lapis lazuli at the entrance, variegated marble columns separating alcoves along two of the walls and decorated panels on the ceiling and the lunettes. The musicians, now busily tuning their instruments, were seated on a small balcony at the far end of the ballroom above two doors leading to a smaller chamber where long tables covered with white cloths suggested that this was where supper would be served later in the evening.

When Jane found herself searching the faces of the men, looking for Devlin, she shook her head and stopped at once. What was the matter with her? She did *not* want to see the man who had so cruelly disappointed her. No, she was much more than disappointed, she was disillusioned. The fact that she had been, without willing it, looking for him, disturbed her further, making her realize he still had the power to hurt her. Hurt her terribly.

"Miss Sterling."

Startled from her unhappy reverie, she turned and saw Claude LaSalle smiling at her. "May I have the honor of being your partner for the first dance of the evening?" he asked, offering her his arm. "You will notice," he added, "I attempt to speak in the English manner."

The orchestra played a fanfare as Claude led her onto the floor. The room hushed. Her color heightened as she felt all eyes on her. Then the waltz began and Claude whirled her away, whirled her around and around, the two of them the only dancers, the circle of watching guests passing by her in a blur of color with Jane more aware of the music than of her partner, yielding to the lilting rhythm of the waltz.

Others began to dance and soon the floor was crowded with waltzing couples. Claude, though he alternated between murmuring compliments to her and nodding to other guests as they danced by, seemed oddly distracted, his thoughts obviously elsewhere. She wondered why but, caught up in the exhilaration of the dance, she put it from her mind.

Then she saw *him* and suppressed a startled gasp. He stood beside a white-haired, hawk-nosed gentleman near one of the marble columns along the near side of the room. Although he nodded from time to time as his companion spoke, all the while he watched her.

He was dressed in black except for a white cravat, almost as if, she thought, he was in mourning. She looked away at once only to have her gaze, seemingly of its own volition, return to him. He gave no sign of greeting or even of recognition but he continued to stare at her so intently she felt a rising discomfiture and resolutely turned her gaze away.

The dance over, Claude escorted her to Estelle who was seated in one of the alcoves. "You are an enchantress," he murmured as he kissed Jane's hand. "If only I were free to enjoy every dance with you but, alas, my guests—" He gestured vaguely toward the room behind him. "I observe, however," he said, glancing at a group of young men clustered near them, "that you shall not lack for partners. My loss is their good fortune."

Jane danced with short young men, with tall young men, handsome men, ugly men, men of charm and men without, graceful men and awkward men. And always she was aware that *he* was there, standing alone now, still watching her, like a nemesis, as though he represented her fate, waiting patiently for her, unable or unwilling to leave her and yet for some reason reluctant to confront her.

Jane tried to ignore him and could not; his presence caused her an unease mingled with an emotion she could not precisely identify, an exasperation perhaps, a sense of futility, of lost hopes and shattered dreams. She would not admit to anticipation for what could there be to look forward to with Devlin?

Later, as she danced from partner to partner in a quadrille, she glanced around the room but did not see Devlin. Again she looked and again failed to find him. Devlin was gone, there could be no doubt about it. She drew in a deep breath, letting it out with a sigh she told herself was relief, all the while knowing deep within herself that the sigh was one of disappointment.

The dance over, the fair-haired young man who had been her partner asked, "Would you enjoy a glass of punch, Miss Sterling?" When Jane nodded, he said, "Pray wait here," leaving her beneath an archway at the rear of one of the alcoves.

"Jane."

Her breath caught at the sound of the oh-so-familiar voice. Devlin's voice. She bit her lip, refusing to look at him.

His hand gripped her wrist. "I came to warn you," he said, his voice urgent.

"Warn me? You came to warn me?" Pulling her hand free, she whirled to face him. "Why must you warn me, Lord Devlin?" she demanded angrily. "What mischief have you planned for me now?" Her voice, she realized belatedly, was much too loud.

He glanced right and left, making her uncomfortably aware that several guests had paused in their conversations to stare quizzically at them.

"I intend you no mischief," he said, "I give you my word. Come with me, if only for a moment." He inclined his head in the direction of the deserted entryway behind them. "Please, Jane." She had never heard him sound so contrite. Or, and this was undoubtedly nearer the truth, pretending to be so contrite.

Reluctantly—she was well aware she might soon regret her decision—she allowed Devlin to escort her from the alcove into a hallway. When he stopped beside a tall pendulum clock, she looked up into his brown eyes, eyes gazing intently at her, and she thought she recognized pain in their depths. She waited, caught as though in a tableau, acutely aware of Devlin standing next to her, Devlin who had never seemed so achingly handsome, all the while listening to the clock ticking off the minutes and, from a distance, the melodic refrain of a waltz.

He leaned to her. For a moment, only a moment, she thought he meant to kiss her, and she held, transfixed and breathless, only to have him straighten, breaking the spell.

"Only this morning," he said, "I received word from London warning me of your friend, M. Claude LaSalle. He happens to be a member of a group of Parisian conspirators seeking to return Napoleon to power in France."

And therefore, Jane realized, Devlin's enemy. Annoyed because she had suspected he meant to kiss her when that had not been his intent at all, she reminded herself she had meant to give Devlin a comeuppance and now Devlin himself was suggesting the perfect way to do it. Giving the cloak to M. LaSalle would devastate Devlin.

"Why should M. LaSalle's politics concern me?" she asked.

He stared at her as though not believing what he had heard her say. "Because Napoleon was a tyrant and will be again if he ever succeeds in once more ruling France. The man wants to be master not only of Europe but of Asia and, if possible, the world as well. Consider how many thousands of men have died on the battlefields of Europe or in engagements at sea because of this one man, think of how much suffering his mania for power has caused. What sort of a world would we be living in today were it not for the steadfastness of England and the heroic resistance of Russia?"

"Yet the wars are over and Europe is at peace. And M. LaSalle is residing in the Sussex countryside, not in France or on Elba. How can he, being in England, possibly help Napoleon to escape?"

"An excellent question for which I have a highly plausible answer. Here we have a Frenchman plotting the return of Napoleon who suddenly leaves France and takes up residence in, of all places, Sussex. Why? For one reason and one reason only." He paused. "That reason is the King's Cloak."

Jane's ire rose. "The King's Cloak? Do you spend every waking hour thinking of the King's Cloak? The cloak is an obsession with you, Devlin, and so you believe it must be an obsession with everyone around you. It may surprise you to know that Claude"—she used his Christian name deliberately in order to nettle Devlin—"has shown little or no interest in the cloak. *My* cloak."

"The better to mislead you, Miss Sterling. And he has succeeded in misleading you."

"You may be a master of deception, Lord Devlin, but I very much doubt M. LaSalle is."

" 'A master of deception'? I thank you for the compliment," he said testily, "even though I suppose it was not intended as one."

"You happen to be quite right, it was not."

"No matter what you may think of me," he said, "the fact remains that LaSalle must never gain possession of the cloak."

She shrugged. "I fail to understand how the King's Cloak will help free Napoleon."

After glancing toward the ballroom to make certain they were alone, he said, lowering his voice, "I admit I might have misled you slightly by leaving the impression that the cloak in and of itself had great value. The secret the cloak may contain, however, happens to be invaluable. In the hands of LaSalle or one of his cohorts it would be worth more than enough to buy Napoleon's release from Elba and to recruit an army. Is it any wonder that LaSalle came to Sussex?"

Was Devlin finally admitting to the truth? Could she believe him or was this another of his fabrications? "You said 'may contain,' I notice. You must harbor doubts."

"Very little in this world is certain. Both LaSalle and I are relying on information more than a century and a half old. The information could well be inaccurate. Besides, a great deal can change in all those years."

"And undoubtedly has changed. I looked in the lining of the cloak when I returned from London. I found nothing there, nothing at all."

Devlin frowned. "What I seek could be concealed in a very small space."

"And what *is* it you seek, Lord Devlin?" she challenged him.

"That," he said stiffly, "I am not at liberty to reveal to you or to anyone else. No matter how much I might wish to."

So he had not yet told her the entire truth and obviously did not intend to. "Yet I presume you want me to turn the cloak over to you." Her tone was tart.

"I want you to allow me to examine it, nothing more. Being an American, I realize you may have little reason to want to help England despite your new-found ties to this country." He reached for her hand but she drew back, frowning. "You must realize," he said softly, "that I have deep feelings for you, Jane, that I care for you in a very special way."

Her breath caught, her eyes misted. She so wanted to believe him. But could she?

"If not for England," he went on, "then do it for me. Show me where you concealed the cloak."

Her anger welled anew. The cloak, the cloak, the cloak. With Devlin, it was always the cloak that mattered most. How dare he claimed he cared for her "in a very special way" when it was clear he did not.

"Will you, Jane?" he persisted.

She tried to calm her inner tumult and speak calmly. She failed. "You, my dear Lord Devlin," she said, "can go to hell."

He stepped back as though she had struck him. "I fail to understand—" he began, only to stop and shake his head. "Jane, you must believe me! I never deceived you because I wanted to, only because I had to, because it was my duty."

Though the hurt in his voice and the pain in his

eyes tugged at her heart, she drew in a long breath
and folded her arms, refusing to succumb to his wiles.
They may have succeeded once, before she was aware
of his duplicity; they would succeed no longer. She
had been hurt too many times and too painfully by
Lord Devlin.

"I welcomed you to Lyon Hall under false pre-
tenses," she told him in a barely audible voice. "You
told me time and again you wanted the King's Cloak
not for yourself but for me, to help me pay the debts
on the Hall. Those were lies. You made love to me at
the Angel Inn and at the Folly to help you in your
pursuit of the cloak." She saw him shake his head but
plunged on. "And now," she accused, "not satisfied,
you bring a small boy to Lyon Hall to act as your
agent, intending to involve a young innocent in your
schemes."

"This 'young innocent' as you call him is, I suppose, Tommy Boggs."

"Precisely. You, Lord Devlin, have no interest in
Tommy other than to further your own plans. Tommy's
your pawn, nothing more, and if he fails in his mission
you intend to toss him aside."

"Not true," he said. "I have an affection for the boy
and, as for you—"

She was startled when the clock beside them chimed
loudly, drowning his words. A glance at the clock told
her it was midnight.

"Ah, Devlin, there you are. At long last." She saw
the white-haired gentleman from the ballroom approaching them. "I must have started looking for you

before eleven. More than an hour ago." He came to stand at Devlin's side.

"Jane," Devlin said, "this is Lord Lansdowne. Miss Jane Sterling," he told Lansdowne.

"Enchanted," Lansdowne said to her, turning again to Devlin. "That chap LaSalle you asked me to keep an eye on? Our French host?"

"Claude LaSalle," Devlin said. His voice became urgent. "What about him?" he asked.

"Looked everywhere," Lansdowne said. "Even in the kitchen. The man's nowhere to be found. Disappeared into thin air."

"The cloak," Devlin said. "LaSalle has gone to Lyon Hall looking for the King's Cloak."

Thirteen

Devlin put his arm around Lord Lansdowne's shoulders, thanking the older man for his help as he walked him back into the ballroom. Leaving Lansdowne, he returned to Jane. "Well, I was right," he said matter-of-factly. "Just as I suspected, our friend LaSalle *is* after the cloak."

Jane was taken aback by his calm demeanor. She had expected Devlin to lose no time in rushing off in pursuit of the Frenchman but he seemed completely unconcerned by Claude's unexplained absence from the ball. Belatedly she understood the reason for his lack of urgency—he believed she had taken care to hide the cloak and so he was certain that LaSalle's ploy was doomed to failure. Her breath caught as she realized the truth—she *had* hidden the cloak but by returning it to the glass case in the King's Room she had chosen the very place where LaSalle would look first.

Devlin, evidently noticing her consternation, said, "I saw you dancing with LaSalle tonight. Is it possible you told him—?" He shook his head. "No, you never would." Of a sudden he looked sharply at her. "Or

would you? Did you tell him where you hid the
cloak?"

Jane bridled. "I certainly did *not*. I never discussed
the cloak with M. LaSalle tonight."

"Capital. I have, then, nothing to fear from our
host's midnight excursion to Lyon Hall." Devlin looked
thoughtful. "I wonder," he said, "whether tonight's ball
was conceived by LaSalle merely as an excuse to lure
you from Lyon Hall to allow him clear passage to the
cloak. Ah, well, I shall never know the whole story
nor do I particularly care to." He bowed to Jane. "May
I, Miss Sterling," he said, "have the honor of leading
you onto the floor for the next dance?"

This was her chance, Jane told herself, to give
Devlin his comeuppance, a chance she might never
have again. All she had to do was accept his offer to
dance while saying nothing more about the King's
Cloak. There was no need for her to lie to him as he
had so often lied to her, there was no need to deceive
him as he had so often deceived her. Merely by remaining silent she would deliver the cloak into
Claude's hands and so repay Devlin for his deviousness.

But instead of the satisfaction she had expected to
feel, she found herself strangely disturbed and so she
hesitated before answering him. When she saw the
questioning look in his brown eyes she felt a pang so
strong she put her hand over her heart. His fingers
touched her wrist ever so gently. She stared up at him,
delighting, despite herself, in the way a stray lock of

his black hair curled down onto his forehead and admiring the masculinity of his angular face.

"Jane?" he said, impatience in his voice.

She shook her head, bemused and undecided.

"You decline to dance with me?" he asked with annoyance, obviously misinterpreting her gesture. His eyes clouded; she could almost feel his growing anger as she might feel the wind rise before a storm.

He was an impatient man, as she well knew, and prone to anger. He was also a man who would never hesitate to deceive her in his pursuit of what he believed to be a worthy goal. She should have done with him now, allow LaSalle to recover the cloak, show Devlin she was not someone to be trifled with.

But she could not, she realized with dismay, not now, not ever.

Because the truth was she'd fallen in love with him. He had deceived her and he might very well deceive her in the future, but whether she willed it so or not she loved him and, because she loved him, she forgave him. She had no other choice but to give her love freely and without condition to Devlin. Only time would tell whether he loved her in return or whether his interest in her was merely a stratagem to take the King's Cloak from her. Many times in the past she had thought that this was his true motive and even now she could not put aside her suspicions. Even so, she forgave him.

Because she loved him. And since she loved him, she could not withhold the truth.

"If M. LaSalle," she told Devlin, "has gone to Lyon

Hall, as you believe he has, he will most certainly find the cloak."

"How is that possible?" Devlin's voice showed his disbelief. "Unless you did tell him where it was after all."

Jane shook her head. "No, I never told him but what I did do, unfortunately, was put the real cloak on the tailor's dummy in the King's Room because I knew you would never think to look there. M. LaSalle, though, has never had reason to doubt that the real cloak was on display there and will find it at once."

She paused, wondering whether it was possible she had put the cloak in the King's Room because, without admitting the truth to herself, she had wanted LaSalle to have it in order to thwart Devlin? But surely she could not be that devious.

"If M. LaSalle really does want the cloak badly enough to steal it," she said as much to herself as to Devlin.

"He does," Devlin said, turning on his heel. "I have not the slightest doubt he does," he added as he started to stride away from her.

Jane ran after him, grasping his arm. He swung around to face her.

"Are you going to Lyon Hall?" she asked him.

He gently but firmly removed her hand from his arm. "I am, though I have little hope of overtaking him."

"What if M. LaSalle returns here once he has the cloak?"

"Would you return here if you were in his place?" Devlin demanded.

Reluctantly, Jane shook her head, realizing that if she wanted the cloak as desperately as Claude LaSalle appeared to want it, she would never risk returning to Montcalm House.

"I intend to go with you to Lyon Hall," she told him.

He started to shake his head but then, changing his mind, Devlin nodded. "Very well," he said, taking her by the arm, "I have Lansdowne's curricle here." As he led her to a door at the side of the house, he looked at her gown. "The night air is cold," he warned. "As they say in the country, the smell of snow is in the air."

She pulled her shawl more closely about her. "But the drive is short," she said.

He opened the door and together they hurried toward the rear of the house. After handing Jane into the curricle, Devlin untethered the matched greys and swung up beside her. Flicking the reins, he urged the horses forward and the curricle rattled along the graveled drive past the brightly lighted windows at the side of the house, into the sweep and onto the avenue leading to the high road, the glow from the Chinese lanterns showing them the way.

Jane sat close beside Devlin as the curricle raced ahead, one hand clutching her shawl and the other holding tight to the rail at her side. The cold, damp November wind bit into her face, bringing tears to her eyes, while high overhead dark clouds drifted across the full moon.

Acutely conscious of Devlin, feeling both comforted by his warmth and disturbed by his presence, she now and again glanced covertly at him, watching as he leaned forward, his gaze intent on the shadowed road ahead. All at once she recalled a verse from the Bible, from the Book of Ruth, and, as they left the avenue and slowed to turn onto the darker Midhurst road she murmured the words to herself: "For whither thou goest, I will go; and where thou lodgest, I will lodge: thy people shall be my people, and thy God my God." The truth of the words, applied to Devlin and herself, seemed to penetrate to the very marrow of her bones, leaving her shaken.

"LaSalle may leave Lyon Hall by this road," Devlin said. "We may be able to intercept him, there is a chance, though a small one."

Bringing her attention back to the matter at hand, she asked, "Where do you expect him to go if he finds the cloak?"

She felt Devlin shrug his shoulders. "More than likely south to one of the Channel ports where he in all probability has a boat waiting to carry him to France. But to which port? Chichester? Portsmouth? Brighton? Dover? Or one of a hundred others? My information from London is that all that can be expected from M. LaSalle is that he will do the unexpected."

Leaving the high road, they drove between the twin lions guarding the entrance to Lyon Hall and on into the woods. After a few minutes Jane saw the dark silhouette of the hall ahead of them. Disappointingly, they had passed no other carriages on their short journey and now, as they approached Lyon Hall, her hopes fell even further when she saw no evidence of activity either on the grounds or in the dimly lit Hall itself.

Bringing the curricle to a halt, Devlin leaped to the ground, strode to the front door and threw it open. Jane climbed down from her seat and followed him. When she entered the Hall, Devlin was nowhere to be seen but as she crossed the entrance hall he appeared in the doorway to the drawing room. She could tell from the grim look on his face that they had arrived too late.

"Come with me," he said, turning and walking across the drawing room.

She followed him to the archway leading to the King's Room.

"As you can see," he said, "the case is empty, the cloak is gone."

Jane clenched her fists in anger. Claude LaSalle had violated her trust by stealing into her home and taking the cloak, her cloak. Her first impulse was to urge Devlin to do all in his power to recover the cloak but, as her anger slowly ebbed, she felt a strange sense of relief. The cloak had brought her nothing but trouble; with the cloak gone, perhaps fortune would smile on her, perhaps she and Devlin could begin anew.

"What will you do now?" she asked him.

He raised his hands in a rueful gesture. "LaSalle might have driven south on any one of a score of roads

.fter he left here." She could tell he was struggling to ‌keep a sense of hopelessness from his voice. "I intend ‌o try to put myself in his place and guess his desti-nation."

He stared at the glass case, muttered something un-der his breath, then walked to the wall and pounded his fist against the paneling, making the pictures jump ‌and sway. "And to think I was so close," he said.

"The fault was mine," she said softly.

Devlin drew in a deep breath. When he turned to her, she saw a muscle twitch in his cheek so she went ‌o him and took his hand in both of hers. He drew her ‌o him, holding her close, so close she could feel the warmth of his body and hear the beating of his heart. With a silent sigh of contentment she closed her eyes, ‌nestling her face against his chest.

After a long moment, Devlin held her away from ‌him, his steady gaze, as it always did, disconcerting ‌her. "No," he said, "the fault was mine and mine alone. I should have told you the truth at the very ‌beginning rather than doing all I could to be clever. If ever a man was hoist by his own petard, I was."

"There are more important things in life than the King's Cloak," she said.

When Devlin made no reply she shook her head ever so slightly, despairing. Probably he did consider the cloak all-important, certainly his actions to date indicated he did. Why should she expect him to sud-denly change now?

Devlin put his hand on her arm and led her to the settee, sitting beside her. "Before I leave for the Channel coast," he said, "I intend to tell you the truth about the King's Cloak."

How much heartache could have been avoided if he had not waited so long.

"The English crown jewels are at the bottom of it all," he said, "those magnificent symbols of our monarchy."

Jane blinked. "The crown jewels? The regalia used during the coronations of your kings and queens."

Devlin nodded. "As you might expect, the jewels are always heavily guarded because of their great value. The crowns and the scepters, the diadems, orbs and swords, the spurs and bracelets and the maces and annointing spoons are adorned with some of the rarest and most valuable precious stones in all the world."

"In the United States of America, we have no crown jewels," she said.

"George Washington's officers urged him to become king," Devlin told her. "He refused. Your country would be better off if he had accepted."

She shook her head vigorously. "We fought the Revolution to escape tyranny, not to re-establish it. As for the crown jewels, imagine all the good that could be done if the jewels were sold and the money put to use helping the deserving poor."

"Sell the crown jewels?" He stared at her as though she had been guilty of a terrible blasphemy. "Have you no sense of tradition, no sense of history? In any event, the jewels belong to the king, not to the people."

She chose not to argue with him. "I think I can guess what you intend to tell me," she said. "Could it be that some of the crown jewels were stolen during your civil war?"

"Rather the opposite," Devlin said. "Instead of being stolen, some of the jewels were saved by royalists when the enemies of the crown sought to take possession of them. After Charles I was made prisoner during our Civil War, the Parliament ordered the crown jewels seized. By a stroke of good fortune some of the jewels had been removed from the collection a short time before to be reset into a royal scepter. Supporters of the king took those jewels—there were diamonds, sapphires, rubies and pearls—and entrusted them to Neil Merriweather with instructions to deliver them to Charles's son who had fled to France. So Merriweather rode south from London with the jewels, intending to cross the Channel to Paris."

Jane nodded eagerly. "But the jewels could never have reached France. If they had, neither you nor LaSalle would have any interest in the King's Cloak."

"Precisely. Cromwell's men soon learned of the missing jewels and pursued Merriweather into Sussex. Fearing capture, Merriweather hid the Stuart jewels and then wrote directions for finding them. He divided these directions into two parts, leaving one in England concealed in what came to be known as the King's Cloak and taking the other with him when he escaped to France. Undoubtedly he meant to tell the king's son where the jewels were hidden—the written record was merely a precaution. A wise one, as it turned out."

"And you have only half of the directions."

"Unfortunately, yes. Shortly after arriving in Paris

and before meeting with the King's son, Merriweather died of natural causes, leaving behind a journal written in a rather simple code and a paper containing a jumble of letters and numbers. The journal meant nothing to the French at the time since they had no knowledge of Merriweather's mission. For some reason they placed the journal in the municipal archives where it was discovered after our occupation of Paris earlier this year."

"I take it the French became aware of the importance of this journal at the same time."

"They must have, otherwise Claude LaSalle would never have come to Sussex. The journal was unearthed by a French clerk who may have made a copy. Or perhaps a French spy had access to the journal at some time."

Jane considered this a moment or two before saying, "Even if M. LaSalle has found and deciphered the second half of Merriweather's directions, the ones hidden in the cloak, he will still have to recover the jewels. They could be cached anywhere between here and London. So you may have time to overtake him after all."

Devlin shook his head. "What I expect LaSalle to do—what I would do if I were in his place—is to depart England as swiftly as possible, sail to France where he can have the cloak thoroughly examined and, if it does conceal the missing half of the directions for finding the jewels, have Merriweather's instructions decoded. The French will then recover the jewels at their leisure, spirit them out of England, sell them and use the proceeds to finance Napoleon's return to power."

Jane frowned as she sought to find a flaw in Devlin's logic and was disappointed when she could not. He had, however, confided in her at last; she was convinced he had now revealed the real reason for his journey to Sussex. But, she also realized, he had admitted to the truth only after learning he had little or no chance to recover the cloak.

"And now?" she asked.

"I propose to take a stab in the dark, try to guess where along the Channel coast LaSalle is bound and drive there myself." He rose and, taking a thick folded packet from his pocket, walked to the deal table where he opened the packet and removed a much-creased paper. "This is a map of southern England," he told her.

She watched as Devlin spread the map on the table and, putting thumb and forefinger to his chin, stood looking down at it. "Where will he go?" he asked himself. With his finger, he traced an imaginary route from Lyon Hall across the South Downs to the coast. "There are so many possibilities. Will he choose Portsmouth? Chichester? Bognor Regis? Littlehampton? Worthing? Brighton? Newhaven? Seaford?"

Hearing a mewing, Jane glanced away from Devlin and saw Chatter standing on the window seat gazing out into the dark. Until very recently the cat had spent the nights comfortably curled in her basket in the warm kitchen. Ever since Tommy Boggs's arrival, though, Chatter had been sleeping in the boy's room.

"Eastbourne?" Devlin said as he went on with his litany of coastal cities and towns. "Hastings? Folkestone? Dover?"

Leaving Devlin's side, Jane crossed the room and opened the window for Chatter. The cat looked outside but instead of leaping from the window seat to the ground, as he often had in the past, he turned and jumped to the floor where he gave Jane one last glance before running past Devlin into the King's Room. Jane shook her head, puzzled by the cat's strange behavior.

Returning to Devlin, she said, "Have you decided on a city?"

He shook his head. "If only I had a clue where he went," he said. "As it is, I might as well decide by blindfolding myself and sticking a pin in the map. If you, Jane, had a choice of a port along the coast, where would you go?"

She studied the map. "Bognor Regis, I believe, but not for any logical reason. Only because the name sounds so odd."

Devlin raised his eyebrows slightly. "As good a reason as any, I suppose." He looked up when a yowl came from the King's Room. "What ails that cat?" he asked.

"He may be sick," Jane said. "I never knew him to act this way before."

Again she left Devlin, walking into the next room where she found Chatter pacing back and forth in front of the glass case. When Jane came to stand behind him, the cat reached up and clawed at the door to the case.

"What are you trying to do, Chatter?" Jane asked. "Whatever is the matter? Did you see a mouse?"

When Chatter persisted in scratching at the door,

Jane went to him, scooping him up into her arms and stroking his velvety fur. The cat purred as he nestled against her but his gaze remained fixed on the case. "The cloak is gone," she told him. "Look, there's nothing inside the case for you."

Glancing into the case, she saw there was, in fact, a small sheet of paper on the floor. Putting Chatter on a chair, she opened the case and picked up the paper, frowning as she stared at a sketch with a single word printed beneath it. At first she was puzzled but all at once she gasped, thinking she understood the picture's meaning.

"Look, Devlin," she said, returning to the drawing room.

He glanced up from his map. "What have you there?" he wanted to know.

After she handed him the paper, he held it to the light. "This seems to be a child's drawing of a team of horses pulling a carriage in a snow storm," he said. "Something is printed below picture in a rather awkward script. 'Handsl'? What in the world does that mean?"

"If I understand the sketch correctly," she said, "it means we may have a chance to overtake M. LaSalle. Not a good chance but a chance nonetheless."

Devlin's doubting glance told her he thought she had taken leave of her senses. "But this drawing of a carriage has nothing to do with LaSalle," he objected.

"Ah," she said, "but it does. Shortly after you brought Tommy Boggs to Lyon Hall, I discovered his father had been an artist and that Tommy had inherited at least some of his skill. He drew a picture of a horse for me, a rather crude horse to be sure, but still recognizable. And that horse happened to be very much like these horses." She nodded at the paper. "Tommy drew this sketch and left it in the glass case for us to find when we discovered the cloak missing."

Devlin studied the picture more carefully. "Tommy, then," he said slowly, "must have meant this as a message to you. The carriage could be LaSalle's, perhaps Tommy saw him ride off. But why would Tommy leave you a picture when he could just as easily wait for your return and tell you what he saw?"

"Because Tommy is no longer at Lyon Hall."

Devlin frowned. "I take it you think he went with LaSalle."

"I do. I suspect he's secreted himself in LaSalle's carriage much as he did when he stowed away on yours in London."

"This picture tells you all that?" Devlin asked, unable to hide his incredulity. "I see nothing of the sort. Have I missed something? Am I dense?"

" 'Handsl' must be Tommy's way of spelling Hansel. Do you remember the story of Hansel and Gretel? The brother and sister were taken into the woods by their stepmother and abandoned there but they left a trail of bread crumbs to show them the way home. Crumbs that were eaten by birds."

"Of course." Devlin struck the heel of his palm against his forehead. "The boy has hidden aboard LaSalle's carriage and plans to leave a trail for us to follow. That small projection in the picture at the rear of the carriage must be Tommy's hand and what I took for snowflakes are whatever he intends to scatter along the road. Do you agree?"

Jane nodded. "I do. But I could well be wrong," she admitted.

"Yet Tommy's sketch offers the only chance to retrieve the King's Cloak." He folded the map and put it in his pocket as he strode to the doorway. "I have no time to lose."

"Devlin!" she said sharply.

He stopped and turned, frowning. After a moment the frown faded and he smiled, holding out his hand to her. "I keep forgetting," he said softly. "Come with me. *We* have no time to lose."

Fourteen

After making certain that Tommy was indeed no longer at Lyon Hall, Jane sent word to Estelle telling her she was leaving with Devlin. Only then did she change into her old grey wool riding costume, complete with jacket, unfashionable but warm.

Devlin, showing his impatience to be on their way, handed her into the curricle and they set off as a distant church bell tolled twice. Feeling a chill breeze from the west, Jane drew her shawl closer about her. Looking overhead, she saw that the clouds now covered the moon and the stars. Though Devlin had hung lanterns on either side of the front of the curricle, they were forced to proceed slowly along the dark avenue beneath the trees.

"We shall soon know whether Tommy succeeded in leaving a trail," Devlin said as they drove between the lions at the gate.

Jane saw him lean forward as he peered into the night; she could almost feel his tenseness. She tried not to care that once again he had forgotten her in his desire to find the cloak but she failed. Obtaining the cloak was more than a desire with him, it amounted to a mania that excluded everything else, including her.

Devlin reined in as soon as they drove onto the Midhurst road. Swinging from the curricle to the ground, he unhooked one of the lanterns and, as she held her breath, walked a short distance to the right, toward Montcalm House, holding the lantern low to the ground. He shook his head.

Returning, he walked along the road in the other direction, south toward the Downs and the Channel. All at once he stopped. Kneeling, he placed the lantern on the road and then reached down to pick up something from the hard-packed surface.

He stood and strode back to the carriage, holding his closed fist aloft. "You were right, Jane," he said with elation in his voice. "Look what I found."

He opened his hand and in the light from the lantern she saw several small pieces of paper on his palm. Her heart leapt joyfully; Tommy had done exactly what his sketch had promised. Tommy was not only talented, he was bold and clever as well. But he was only a child, a child who had placed himself in danger. She devoutly hoped no harm would befall him.

"These scraps are from the pages of a book," Devlin said excitedly. "Tommy must have taken a book with him when he smuggled himself aboard LaSalle's coach and intends to rip it apart and strew pieces of paper behind them as they drive toward the coast."

"Seldom has a book been put to better use."

He glanced at her as though suspecting her of insincerity, but she meant each and every word. By now she was almost as eager to find the King's Cloak as he was, though not for the same reason. She simply wished the search to be over and done with once and for all.

Devlin looked anxiously up at the overcast sky. "We must pray the snow holds off," he said. "Even a flurry would cover Tommy's trail of paper scraps and allow LaSalle to make good his escape."

Climbing into the curricle, he put his arm around Jane's shoulders, hugging her. "We stand a fair chance to recover the King's Cloak," he said, "thanks to Tommy Boggs. What a clever lad!" He paused. "And thanks to you, of course," Devlin added.

To Jane, Devlin's belated praise was almost worse than none at all. Must it always be the cloak, the King's Cloak? Did Devlin's thoughts ever stray from the cloak, even for an instant?

Her exhilaration at discovering Tommy's message and finding his trail of scraps of paper faded as they drove slowly through the night. The breeze was cold, the curricle unsuited to night driving in the winter, their pace was slow, she was tired and, because of what she considered to be Devlin's single-minded pursuit of the cloak, she soon found herself on the edge of despair.

They made their painstaking way through Midhurst with Devlin alighting at each intersection to search for more of Tommy's scraps of paper. Leaving the village, their pace, though still slow, increased as they drove several miles without coming to a crossroads.

"LaSalle continues to surprise me," Devlin told her.

"I expected him to veer to the east at the first opportunity but no, he appears headed directly across the South Downs to Chichester. He must be trying to confound me by choosing the obvious port just as you tried to do by hiding the cloak in the King's Room."

Tried to confound you? I not only tried, Jane thought indignantly, I succeeded. But she said nothing.

When, some hours later, the sky reluctantly began to brighten in the east they were driving over the Downs, a succession of rolling hills stretching for many miles across southern Sussex. Jane glanced up and saw that clouds hung low and leaden over their heads and the smell of snow was in the air.

"A penny for your thoughts," Devlin said, making Jane realize how quiet she had been during the drive.

For a time she said nothing as she attempted to bring order from the jumble of thoughts in her mind. "I was wondering," she said at last, "what would happen if we did recover the King's Cloak."

"Why, I would do my best to find the missing part of the coded message. If I did find it, I would proceed to solve the code if I possibly could."

She nodded, having gotten that far herself. "Assuming you decoded the message and were able to find the hiding place of the Stuart jewels, what then?"

"My only possible course of action would be to return the jewels to their rightful owner, to King George or, since the king is in seclusion, to the Prince Regent."

Jane frowned. "And what do you think he would do with them?" she persisted.

Devlin stared at her. "What a strange question. The

Prince would see to it that they take their place with the other crown jewels in the Jewel Office at the Tower of London. What led you to ask?"

"From what I read in the London newspapers," Jane said, "the Prince Regent is always desperately in need of money. For Carlton House, for his fetes and parties, for new parks, new streets, and new terraces in London and a pleasure palace of sorts in Brighton. I wondered if he might be tempted to sell some of the jewels rather than ask a reluctant Parliament for more money."

"What odd notions you Americans have. The Prince would no more think of selling some of the crown jewels than—" Devlin paused. "Than I would consider keeping the jewels for myself."

Devlin, Jane decided, had an extraordinarily high opinion of English royalty, evidently considering them exempt from the frailties of mere mortals. Though she had a much more jaundiced view, she decided to say nothing. Americans, he would say, failed to understand the English. Perhaps he was right, perhaps not. True, her views would never quite coincide with his yet she had come to like the people she had met since arriving in England and, as for Lyon Hall, it would break her heart to leave the home of her forebears.

A few minutes later, Devlin brought the curricle to a halt. When she looked a question at him, he said, "As far as I could tell, there have been no scraps of paper on the road for at least a mile. LaSalle may have turned off at that last crossroads."

Devlin swung the curricle into the entrance to a lane, turned about and started to retrace their route.

Here there were few trees, the road running between fields where the grass was still green. Jane had not seen any sign of habitation for the last several miles.

Something cold and moist struck her cheek. A snow-flake? A glance up at the grey sky told her nothing but when she looked to the west, above the gentle slopes of hills where sheep seemed to be making their way toward the bottomland, she saw what looked like a white mist. Snow. A moment later several more flakes drifted from the sky to land and melt on her shawl.

"Damnation," Devlin muttered, "snow." He flicked the reins to urge the greys on. "I only hope the snow keeps melting as soon as it lands. It should, the ground is still warm."

When they came to the crossing, an unmarked intersection of two dirt roads, Devlin swung the curricle onto the one leading toward the east, slowing the pace of the horses as he scanned the roadway. The only sounds were the steady clip-clop, clip-clop of the horses' hooves and the faint ting-tang, ting-tang of sheep bells.

"Ah," he said, pointing ahead of them, "I see Tommy's trail of paper. This is the way they went." He shook his head. "Though I have no idea where LaSalle might be headed since, to the best of my knowledge, this road swings north after a few miles, heading away from the coast rather than toward it."

Again Devlin increased their pace. Jane pulled her shawl closer as the snow fell faster than before with the whirling flakes large and moist. While the first flakes had melted on striking the ground, these later ones did not. Soon the road was white.

"We can only hope and pray," Devlin said to her, "that LaSalle stays on this road." Peering through the falling snow, he suddenly groaned. "I see another crossroad ahead of us," he said. "Should I guess which way to go? Should I toss a coin? We have one chance in two of being right."

He brought the curricle to a stop and Jane saw that one road branched away to the right, the other to the left. She shook her head, sighing. How could they possibly tell which way to go? she wondered.

As she looked first along one road and then the other searching for a clue she noticed that the first heavy flurry of snow had subsided to be replaced by a steady fall of smaller flakes that whitened her bonnet and shawl while it dampened her face. Gazing through the falling snow, she drew in a sharp, astonished breath.

"What in the world could that be?" she asked. "Do you see that strange sight off to our left on the far side of that next hill?"

Devlin held up his hand to his forehead to shield his eyes from the snow. "It looks for all the world like the dome of a building," he said, "though I have no idea who would erect a domed building here on the South Downs. Perhaps what we see is a Folly of some sort."

"Just now," she said, "I was almost certain I saw the dome move ever so slightly."

"As did I. We had best drive that way and have a look."

Devlin turned the horses to the left and they drove a few hundred feet in the direction of the dome. As they neared the crest of the hill, he swung horses and carriage off the road into a field. "Wait for me here," he told Jane as he climbed from the curricle to the ground and started walking up the gentle incline.

Ignoring Devlin's admonishment to stay where she was—he seemed to have difficulty understanding she would *not* be stored for safe keeping—Jane left the curricle and followed him up the low hill to the crest, careful not to slip on the light coating of snow. As she walked up beside him, he was staring down into the valley.

"Unbelievable." He glanced at her, shaking his head. "I might have expected to see this in Hyde Park or elsewhere in London but never here on the South Downs."

Looking through the curtain of falling snow, Jane gasped at what she saw. The white dome was in actuality the top of a huge blue balloon lightly covered by snow, a balloon tethered by four stout ropes leading to stakes that had been driven into the ground. M. LaSalle, who was wearing the King's Cloak and a tri-cornered hat, paced in front of the balloon's basket, his arms folded as he gazed above him first at the balloon and then at the steadily falling snow. His coach and four waited a short distance away; Tommy Boggs, however, was nowhere to be seen. Where could he be? she asked herself worriedly.

"LaSalle will never dare make an ascent in this weather," Devlin said. "If the storm lasts for a half hour more, he'll be forced to give up this idea of making his escape by air."

LaSalle, Jane saw, was not alone. Five other men watched him, perhaps waiting for his orders. One wore an oversized black coat and a top hat, the other four were roughly garbed. Those four were, Jane suspected, farm laborers. All of the men had been mantled in white by the snow.

"That man in the black coat and the top hat standing near the mechanical apparatus with all the hoses," Jane said. "What do you suppose he does?"

"He must be an expert balloonist hired by LaSalle to inflate the balloon by feeding hydrogen into the envelope and then to pilot the craft. As you can see, the balloon's already fully inflated so they must have started their preparations before dawn. The balloonist appears to be French while the four others seem to be helpers, probably men recruited from a nearby village."

"You said we should expect the unexpected from M. LaSalle," Jane reminded him.

Devlin smiled. "Fate has been kind to us," he said. "Just when all seemed lost, LaSalle has been delivered into our hands."

Jane stared at him, wondering how Devlin intended to cope not merely with M. LaSalle but with his five hirelings as well. "Perhaps," she suggested, "we should wait until M. LaSalle takes shelter from the storm before we make an attempt to recover the cloak."

Devlin shook his head. "The French, and here we have at least two of them, are not to be trusted, I find them capable of acts of sheer madness. LaSalle might well attempt to fly off in the teeth of this storm." Turning away from the balloon, he took Jane's arm and led her back down the slope to the curricle. "You, Jane," he said, "are to remain here until I return. Do you understand?"

When she nodded, Devlin drew a long-barreled pistol from inside his coat. "This should convince LaSalle to surrender the cloak," he said.

As Jane looked at the pistol, she felt the rapid beating of her heart. Apprehensive, fearful that M. LaSalle might also be armed, she reached to Devlin and touched his hand, the hand holding the pistol.

"Be careful," she said, making no effort to dissuade him, knowing he firmly believed he had no choice but to face the overwhelming odds against him.

Devlin leaned to her, kissing her quickly, his lips cool on hers, like the touch of a snowflake. Starting to turn away, he suddenly held, reaching out and taking her in his arms, his lips finding hers in a long and passionate kiss. Releasing her, he strode away up the slope, the pistol held at his side, and disappeared over the crest, leaving her staring after him, bemused.

Determined to know what was happening, Jane climbed into the curricle, took the reins and flicked them until the horses reluctantly plodded up the slope. Stopping at the crest, where she intended to wait for

Devlin, she looked through the gently falling snow into the valley.

Devlin, she saw, was striding confidently down the hill toward the balloon, all the while keeping Claude LaSalle's coach between himself and the Frenchman; neither M. LaSalle nor any of the other men had seen him as yet. M. LaSalle had used a rope ladder to climb into the balloon's basket, the four laborers were untying the ropes tethering the balloon to the ground while the man in the top hat stood in front of the basket gesticulating at LaSalle, evidently trying to dissuade him from ascending during the storm.

As she watched Devlin skirt around the coach, her breath caught. Tommy! She had temporarily forgotten the boy. He must, she assured herself, still be hiding in LaSalle's coach. Devlin, in his desire to seize the cloak, had given no thought to Tommy's whereabouts. Was Tommy in the coach? She *must* find out.

Jane climbed down from her seat in the curricle and, after looping the reins around the branch of a bush, hurried down the hill. She heard Devlin's voice coming from beyond the coach but she was unable to make out his words. Looking cautiously past the coach she saw him, pistol raised, shouting at LaSalle. The man in the top hat stood to one side with a startled look on his face while the four others had finished untying the mooring ropes and were now straining to hold the balloon in place.

Jane quickly climbed the steps on the side of LaSalle's coach and peered inside. The coach was empty. She hesitated, wondering where Tommy could be. Had he dropped from the coach and concealed himself nearby? Or might he be in the boot? Hastening to the rear of the coach, she lifted the lid of the storage compartment.

The boy, holding the remnants of a book in one hand, grinned up at her.

"Tommy!" she cried. "Thank God." Jane took his hand and helped him scramble from the boot to the ground. He gazed up at the balloon.

"Gor," he said. "I never seen the like."

"Our curricle," Jane said, grasping his hand, "is at the top of the hill." She meant to take Tommy there and wait for Devlin's return.

"Look!" Tommy shouted.

She turned to see that two of the laborers no longer held mooring ropes; one had dropped his rope on the ground while the other had rewrapped his around the stake. Both were now cautiously stalking Devlin from the rear. Devlin, motioning to LaSalle with the pistol, was unaware of the danger threatening him.

"Quick," Jane told Tommy. "Those men at the ropes are English. We must tell them not to let the balloon ascend, make them keep the Frenchman here by warning them he's Napoleon's agent."

Jane ran to the right while Tommy veered off to the left.

"Hold them bloody lines," she heard Tommy call out, "the Frog's Boney's man, the Frog's Boney's man." The two men who had been stalking Devlin hesitated.

As Jane ran past the balloon's basket, she saw that M. LaSalle had removed the cloak and seemed about ready to toss it to Devlin. She ran toward the two men who still held fast to the mooring lines.

"Keep the balloon here," she called to them. "The Frenchman's—"

An arm caught her around the waist, yanking her backward. She gasped. Glancing behind her, she saw the top-hatted Frenchman. She struggled to free herself, twisting and turning as she clawed at his encircling arm. In vain—the man's grip tightened.

She looked toward Devlin. He stood with the pistol in one hand while he reached toward the basket for the King's Cloak with the other. The balloon, now held by only two ropes, strained to rise. At any moment, she feared, it would break free, carrying M. LaSalle and the cloak into the unknown.

Tommy shouted. Devlin swung around to look behind him, glanced first at the two men who, appearing confused, had stopped, looked next at Tommy and then at her. Jane scarcely noticed the snow softly falling on the balloon hovering over their heads, scarcely noticed Tommy or the two undecided men or the other two men still holding the mooring ropes. She saw only Devlin, noting the look of surprise and consternation on his face.

Without a moment's hesitation, Devlin ran toward her, calling to the Frenchman to release her. Her captor backed away, his arm still circling her waist as he dragged her with him. Devlin stopped a few feet away, calmly thrust his pistol into a pocket of his coat, then reached past Jane, his hand closing on the Frenchman's neck.

She spun away from her captor, turning in time to see Devlin release his grip on the Frenchman's neck and hit him a stunning blow to the jaw. The Frenchman grunted, staggered back and sprawled on the ground, his hat rolling to one side. He blinked and his hand went to his jaw, but he made no effort to rise.

"Are you safe?" Devlin asked Jane. "Did he harm you? If he did—" He reached down as though ready to lift the quaking Frenchman from the ground and hurl him down again.

Jane shook her head. Devlin, she told herself, Devlin came to me, ignoring the cloak. He chose me! "The cloak," she said. "You must get the cloak."

"The cloak?" It seemed almost as though he had forgotten LaSalle and the cloak.

He nodded, touching her face fleetingly with his fingertips before turning toward the balloon. She looked past Devlin, expecting to see balloon and basket rising into the cloudy sky. But no, the basket, tilting precariously, still was only a few feet above the ground. Now three men held firm to the ropes while the fourth rope dangled free. As she watched, Tommy grabbed the loose rope, clutching it with all his might.

Devlin strode toward the basket with Jane running a few feet behind him.

"Unhand the ropes," M. LaSalle called out to his hirelings. Not one of them obeyed him.

"The cloak," Devlin told LaSalle, again drawing the pistol from his pocket. As Jane watched, he slowly and with great deliberation cocked the gun. She had no doubt he would use it.

M. LaSalle hesitated, staring first at the pistol and then looking at Devlin as though to judge the depth of his resolve. Throwing up his hands in defeat, LaSalle tossed the cloak from the basket to the ground. Jane heard a faint and ragged cheer from behind her. Almost at once the basket started to rise, swaying from side to side as it ascended. When she glanced around, she saw that the three men had released the ropes. Tommy, though, still clinging to his rope, slowly rose into the storm.

Devlin raced across the snow-covered field until he was below the boy. "Tommy," he called, "jump." Looking up at Tommy, looking down to keep his footing, he tried to keep pace with the balloon as it floated eastward.

"Tommy," Jane called, "let go of the rope."

Tommy looked down, his eyes wide with fright. Would he cling to the rope until it was too late? Then he let go and was falling, falling through the snow, falling for an eternity. Devlin caught him in his arms, staggered, recovered and swung the boy safely to the ground as, far above, the balloon rose higher and higher. Tommy, grinning, ran to Jane and threw his arms around her. She hugged him, laughing and crying with relief.

When she looked up she saw that the balloon had disappeared into the haze of the falling snow. Devlin stood a few feet away from her, holding the King's Cloak. Coming to her, he draped the cloak over her shoulders. She smiled, smiled through her tears, warmed not by the cloak but by Devlin's gesture.

Fifteen

"You seem troubled," Devlin said to Jane as they started to drive through the steadily falling snow with Tommy huddled between them.

"He may be a villain," she said, "but I worry about what will become of M. LaSalle and his balloon in this storm."

"You, Jane, are much too tender-hearted. LaSalle took the risk and so must accept the consequences, whatever they are." Devlin's harsh tone softened. "What he will probably do, since he's no fool, is release gas from his balloon and make a descent as soon as he can."

"I do hope so," Jane said. "Losing the cloak was sufficient punishment for him." She peered through the snow. "Where are *we* bound?"

"Since I also try to be no more of a fool than I can help," Devlin told her, "I plan to seek temporary refuge from the storm at the home of a Squire Archibald Hopkins. The four men who helped LaSalle with his balloon are farm laborers employed by tenants of the squire's."

"Happen the squire makes even a farthing squeal," Tommy put in.

"Whatever do you mean?" Jane asked him.

"Overheard the men talking, I did," Tommy said. "The squire, he be a pinch-penny."

Devlin chuckled. "I shall offer to pay for our night's lodging," he said, "if the good squire sees fit to insist. I feel uncommonly generous for today I feel as though I were sitting on top of the world."

When Devlin glanced at her, smiling, Jane's heart lifted in response. Devlin had proven he cared for her, Tommy was safe and they had recovered the cloak. What more could she possibly want from life? she asked herself as they drove slowly over the Downs with the sound of the curricle's wheels muffled by the inch or so of snow on the road. Warmed by these thoughts, she found herself nodding. How terribly tired she was! And how very very happy . . .

When she awakened she felt a wisp of a pleasant dream slipping away. She tried to bring it back but all she could recall were strong arms holding her, carrying her, protecting her. She let herself drift in blissful surrender, half asleep and half awake, savoring the moment. Finally, hearing strange voices, she opened her eyes and found that Devlin was actually carrying her up steps with a house mantled in white looming above her.

"Ah, you're awake," Devlin said, pulling the bell before swinging her carefully down to stand on the porch step, his arm lingering around her waist. As the door opened, she reluctantly edged away from him, straightening her bonnet and shaking the snow from her skirts.

An elderly retainer led them along a dingy hall to the parlor, an equally dim and shabby room, where they were greeted by Squire Archibald Hopkins, a gentleman of middle years whose florid face and button-straining corpulence hinted at a life of over-indulgence.

"More than happy to accommodate you and your American cousin, my lord," the squire said after Devlin had made slightly inaccurate introductions and asked for refuge from the storm.

"My cousin and I appreciate your kindness," Devlin told him. "In London, Sussex is deservedly renowned for its hospitality."

"I expect news of my collection brought you here to the South Downs," the squire said. "I can think of no other good reason for wandering so far afield on such a day as this."

Jane watched in bewilderment as Devlin bowed slightly and said, "When one possesses something both unique and valuable, is it possible to hide the fact even though he happens to reside in Downland? One man tells another, word spreads and before long all of London is abuzz."

She was all but certain Devlin had never heard of Squire Hopkins until this very morning, much less any collection of his. Thinking back over Devlin's words, though, she decided he had really managed to say nothing at all while appearing to say a great deal.

Squire Hopkins beamed with delight. "Your words

do me proud. Would you and your cousin care to see the collection now?"

"We have traveled a considerable distance in an open carriage," Devlin said, "and as a result find ourselves quite fatigued. If we could rest for a few hours we might better appreciate your treasures. Besides having additional time in which to anticipate our forthcoming pleasure."

"As you wish, my lord," the squire said, ringing for a maid to show them to their rooms.

Jane found her bed chamber scarcely warmer than the outdoors. Not only had no fire been lit but none had been laid in the hearth. Deciding she had no choice but to make the best of what she was given, she removed only her boots and bonnet before crawling into the chilly bed, keeping the cloak wrapped around her as she pulled up the none-too-thick comforter. Chilly or not, she immediately sank into sleep.

Awakened by a tapping at her door, she glanced about her, aware that considerable time had passed. "Who is it?" she asked.

"Devlin."

She sat up in bed, aware of how sadly rumpled she must look. It seemed to her that Devlin almost always saw her at her worst. "I've been asleep," she called.

"May I open the door?" he asked.

Her hands fluttered to her hair and she shook her head. There was no way she could quickly put herself to rights. Sighing, she rose and padded across the worn carpet to open the door herself.

Devlin smiled at her from the hall, apparently ignoring her untidiness. "An early dinner will be served within the hour, cousin," he said, "and afterwards we are invited, nay, commanded, to view Squire Hopkins's collection."

"Had you really heard of the collection?" she asked.

"Never, and I still have no notion what the good squire collects. But who could have an objection to giving the squire so much pleasure at no cost to myself?" He paused. "What I came to speak to you about was the cloak, not the collection. I suggest we make no attempt to solve the cloak's secret until we return to Lyon Hall where we can examine it at our leisure. Do you agree?"

"Most readily. Especially since I feel I may freeze in this room should I be forced to remove the cloak. Shall we be returning to Lyon Hall tonight?"

"No, tomorrow morning. The snow has stopped but the hour is late. If we lavish enough praise on his collection, I expect even our pinch-penny squire will offer us a night's lodging."

"What sort of collection do you expect to see?" she asked.

"Sheep bells perhaps, this being the South Downs. Or an array of shepherd's crooks or Sussex-ware. Whatever the case, we shall know before long."

As soon as Devlin left, Jane refreshed herself, smoothed her hair and brushed the wrinkles from her skirts as best she could before hurrying down the stairs to the dining room where she met the squire's wife, a pale, wispy woman who seemed to defer to her husband in all things. Despite her hunger, Jane found the mutton-heavy meal, served in a most lackadaisical fashion by the aged retainer, almost interminable.

"Ah-ha," the squire said, rising when they finished their custard, "and now for the *pièce-de-resistance*. If you, my lord Devlin, and your American cousin will but accompany me."

He led them from the dining room along a hall to the rear of the house. "I had this room built especially to hold my collection," the squire told them as he opened the door and stood to one side.

On entering the room, Jane's first impression was of unaccustomed warmth—a fire blazed in the hearth—her second of glittering light reflecting from glass and metal. Lamps, all brightly lit, were placed strategically about the room, a large room containing row upon row of glass cases. And inside the cases—

"Here you have my collection of snuffboxes!" Squire Hopkins said proudly.

"Amazing," Devlin exclaimed, raising his arms as though in awe. "I never saw the like."

"Extraordinary," Jane said, telling the squire no more than the truth.

There were hundreds of snuffboxes on display, large snuffboxes and small snuffboxes, oval snuffboxes and square snuffboxes, metal snuffboxes and wooden snuffboxes, ornate snuffboxes and plain snuffboxes, old snuffboxes and new snuffboxes, snuffboxes of every conceivable variety.

Squire Hopkins placed his hand on a black-bound book ensconced on a pedestal near the door. "This," he told them, "is the catalog of the collection, a record of each box, where and when purchased, from whom, and the cost. My goal is to possess an example of every type of snuffbox made anywhere in the world, whether in England, France, Italy, or Russia. A costly aim, to be sure, but well worth the expense."

"Your collection is amazing," Devlin told him, "truly amazing. When I return to London, you may be assured I shall sing its praises."

The following day, with the sun rapidly melting the last of the snow, Devlin and Jane drove north over the Downs to Lyon Hall with Tommy once again sitting between them.

"His collection *is* amazing," Devlin said, defending himself to Jane. "How often do you find such a superb collection in such an out of the way spot?"

Jane gave him a speaking look. "His house is cold, dingy, and dilapidated, the grounds are untended, his tenants appear poor, his wife's clothes are threadbare, his servants are a surly lot, and all the while Squire Hopkins spends what little money he has collecting, of all useless things, snuffboxes."

"His money is his to spend as he pleases, you must grant him that. And think of the pleasure his collection will give other snuffbox devotees in years to come after the squire passes on to his reward. Many of his jeweled boxes are akin to works of art worthy of exhibition by the Royal Academy."

She raised her eyebrows in astonishment. "His snuffbox collection may provide pleasure for the few," she said vehemently, "but at the same time it assures misery for the many." About to go on, she looked sharply at Devlin. "Are you funning me?" she asked.

He grinned at her. "Perhaps just a bit. I admit the squire's lust for containers for snuff is satisfied at the expense of all those around him."

"His house weren't no warmer than the London streets," Tommy put in. "I ain't never been so cold inside a place."

Jane, sharing the cloak with Tommy, put an arm around him, drawing him closer to her.

Devlin glanced at them. "I see the King's Cloak is being put to good use. I admit I'm eager to examine it at long last."

As they rattled on, Jane grew more and more troubled. Her brief visit at the home of Squire Hopkins had discomfited her. She sympathized with the squire's wife, his servants, his tenants and even with the squire himself. They were all, she believed, held captive by one man's misguided dream.

Even so, she should be joyful, should she not? They had the King's Cloak, their long search was over. If the cloak truly held the secret Devlin was seeking he would, by one means or another, uncover it and proceed to find the hiding place of the Stuart Jewels.

Why, then, did she feel this touch of sadness? Perhaps, she told herself, because excitement was in the chase, in the seeking, not in the finding. Perhaps because she was still unsure of the depth or constancy of Devlin's affection. Or she could be uneasy because she realized that Devlin, if and when he recovered the

ewels, would hasten to leave Lyon Hall to return them
to the Prince Regent.

Where they rightfully belonged, she reminded herself. Or did they? What had the Prince Regent himself
done to recover these jewels lost for more than a hundred and fifty years? And what would he do once they
were in his possession? He might return them to the
Jewel Office in the Tower as Devlin insisted would be
the case, or he might well use them for his own pur-
poses. She had much less confidence in the Prince's
sense of history and tradition than Devlin obviously
did.

The clatter of the curricle's wheels on the Midhurst
stones brought her out of her unhappy reverie. Looking
past Tommy, she saw the church with its small graveyard nestled against its walls. A well-remembered
poem came to mind and she murmured a few of the
lines:

> " 'Full many a gem of purest ray serene,
> The dark unfathom'd caves of ocean bear:
> Full many a flower is born to blush unseen,
> And waste its sweetness on the desert air.' "

"Elegy Written in a Country Churchyard," Devlin
said. "A rather melancholy poem for my taste."

Jane glanced down at Tommy, who was leaning
against her, and saw he had fallen asleep. "The truth
is often sad," she said, vowing it would not be in
Tommy's case, not if she could prevent it.

Devlin gave her a long look, saying nothing, and they
drove on in silence, soon leaving the Midhurst road to
pass between the stone pillars and along the avenue to

Lyon Hall. As they neared the house, Horatio raced from the stable, barking joyfully at his master's return as he cavorted beside the curricle, while Chatter, sitting at the drawing room window, looked down at the dog's exuberant greeting with apparent disdain.

As soon as they were in the Hall, Devlin led the way to the dining room where Jane took off the blue cloak and spread it on the table. Tommy, holding Chatter in his arms, perched on a chair, watching as she helped Devlin carefully remove the lining and spread it beside the cloak. Jane's heart sank when they found no evidence of a message on either the lining or the cloak. After re-examining the clasp and chain, Devlin shook his head.

"Are you certain we have the right cloak?" he asked.

Jane nodded toward the Cavendish label. "Quite certain. The label is—" She stared at the label, then looked up at Devlin, her eyes widening.

"The label!" they exclaimed in unison.

Devlin used his knife to free the label from the cloak, revealing a piece of yellowed cloth lightly basted into the fold of the label. He removed the cloth and, when he smoothed it with his fingers, Jane saw that it contained a jumble of embroidered letters and numbers.

"Capital," Devlin said, "now we have the other half of Merriweather's directions." Removing the oil skin packet from his coat, he opened it and laid the first part of the directions on the table. "I need a large sheet of paper," he said.

Tommy had left Chatter curled on the chair and had

come to stand on tiptoe to look down at Devlin's find. Now he glanced at Jane. "The book room?" he asked. When she nodded, he ran off in that direction.

"Were you thinking of Tommy Boggs," Devlin asked Jane as soon as they were alone, "when you quoted from the *Elegy* when we passed through Midhurst? Is he, with what you see as his artistic ability, the flower born to bloom unseen?"

"Tommy? Yes," she said, "but not only him. Tommy and all the other boys and girls who never have the chance to make use of their God-given talents because they lack the money or the position or the encouragement of a father or mother. How much happier they might be; how much better England would be served if children with abilities were given half a chance."

"As I have pointed out before, you, Jane, are an idealist. A dreamer of impossible dreams."

"I have no desire to tear down and start anew to rebuild society, I only wish to make what we have a bit better. I would rather be a dreamer, Lord Devlin, than a naysayer."

He stared at her, his brow furrowed. "Is that how you see me, Jane, as a—" He broke off as Tommy ran into the room and laid a sheet of paper on the table.

"How quick you were," Devlin said to the boy. "Now we shall see what, if anything, Mr. Merriweather bequeathed us. First the message recovered in Paris."

He printed the letters and numbers on the paper: D O N E C 6 1

"And next the message embroidered on the cloth hidden in the cloak's label."

He printed the second set of letters and numbers below the first:

T A I L H V 6

"Could it be a code?" Jane asked. "With each letter or number signifying a different letter or number?"

"Possibly, but if it is Merriweather has set us an almost impossible task since there are so few letters in his message to provide clues. I think, and hope, he merely scrambled the letters and numbers of his message to create an anagram. We could begin to solve his puzzle by just considering the letters and not the numbers."

He printed the letters across the paper:

D O N E C T A I L H V

Jane tried to rearrange the letters in her mind. "I can make out some words," she said, "but they make very little sense. I see 'done' and 'tone' and 'late' and 'hone' and 'lone' and 'code' and 'tailed' and 'veil.' And many more, all meaningless."

Devlin frowned. "Solving the anagram could be more complicated than I thought," he said as he started writing various combinations of the letters. "No," he said, shaking his head as he discarded one word after another, "no, no, no."

We seem so close, Jane thought, and yet so far. " 'Lined,' " she suggested, "or 'dial.' "

"Ah-ha," Devlin said. "Using those same letters you just mentioned, I perceive a man's name hidden in this jumble. The name 'Daniel.' "

"Was Merriweather's first name Daniel? Could he be referring to himself?"

"No, his name was Neil, at least I think it was Neil, but it definitely was not Daniel."

"Perhaps someone associated with Merriweather was named Daniel. Or it might be the name of the person he entrusted the jewels to before he left England."

"I read Merriweather's journal rather carefully and I could almost swear on a Bible that the name Daniel was never mentioned, not once. Let me try removing the letters that spell Daniel and see what we have left." He printed the remaining letters:

O C T H V

"October?" Jane suggested.

"I doubt a month would have much significance."

Jane frowned as she concentrated. "A few minutes ago you mentioned a Bible," she said. "Daniel is a book in the Bible and O.T. could stand for the Old Testament." Her voice rose excitedly. "That would make CH the chapter and V would be the verse in that chapter. The numbers six, one and six would be the numbers of the chapter and verse."

Devlin reached over and hugged her. "Splendid. And since there are only twelve chapters in the Book of Daniel and none of those chapters has sixty or more verses, this must mean the Book of Daniel, chapter six, verse sixteen."

Jane was astonished by his intimate knowledge of the Bible. But should she be? Ever since they first met, Devlin had succeeded in surprising her time after time.

"We have a Bible in the library," Jane said.

She and Devlin hurried along the hall with Tommy and Chatter at their heels. Placing the large black-bound volume on the library table, Jane turned the pages until she came to the Book of Daniel.

"This is verse sixteen." She started to read, " 'Then the king commanded, and they brought Daniel, and cast him into the den of lions. Now the king spake and said to Daniel, Thy God whom thou servest continually, he will deliver thee.' "

"We are at *Lyon* Hall," Devlin said thoughtfully. "Our friend Merriweather may simply have meant he left the jewels here. I find it hard to imagine, though, that he intended us to tear down the house and dig up the grounds searching for the jewels. He must have had a specific place in mind. I wonder if the word 'den' has a special meaning?"

"I think the New Testament mentions a den of thieves," Jane said.

"In some places in England," Devlin added, "a glen or a small valley is called a den."

"But a den is usually an animal's lair," Jane insisted. "Might there have been an animal's den on the Lyon property in Merriweather's time? He could have secreted the jewels in a cave, though I know of none hereabouts."

"What if he don't mean Lyon Hall?" Tommy piped up. "You got real lions here, too."

"Real lions?" Devlin raised his eyebrows at the boy. "What real lions are those, Tommy?"

"Them lions beside the road. "There ain't no other real lions."

Jane nodded. "He means the two lions atop the pillars."

"Tommy," Devlin told him, clapping him on the shoulder, "you may very well be on to something. I expect those stone lions were here in Merriweather's time. Shall we organize an expedition and find out?"

Both Tommy and Jane eagerly agreed.

While Devlin and Tommy went to the stable, Jane waited inside the entry hall. She recalled a day long ago when, a young girl, she swam too far from shore and was caught by the river's current. Swept downstream, she had been panic-stricken and helpless, fearing she would drown, until the current veered and she was able to climb atop an outcropping of rocks.

Now, or so it seemed to her, she was once again being swept forward toward an unknown destination. She could only hope and pray she would find a haven at the end of this journey.

Hearing the clatter of the curricle, she looked from the window and saw Devlin and Tommy approaching with a short ladder tied to the back of the carriage.

"While the curricle was being readied," Devlin told Jane when she joined them, "I talked to Tommy of the wonders of the Lansdowne Folly to throw the stable-hands off the scent."

Tommy nodded vehemently. "Foxed 'em proper, we did."

They drove through the woods to the entrance to Lyon Hall where Devlin untied the ladder and placed it against the pillar on the left side of the avenue. Climbing to the uppermost rung, he searched around the base of the lion—the beast rested Sphinxlike on the pillar with his head raised and front legs outstretched.

"Nothing at all," he told them.

After clambering over the recumbent lion, Devlin shook his head. Again nothing. He tried to put his hand in the lion's partly open mouth but it would not fit.

"Tommy," he called down to the boy, "climb up here, my hand's too large."

Tommy clambered up the ladder and shoved his hand into the lion's mouth, his entire arm disappearing from Jane's sight. She held her breath.

"Cor!" Tommy cried, pulling his arm free. He triumphantly held up a worn leather pouch. Jane's heartbeat quickened. Was it possible?

Devlin and Tommy climbed down the ladder to the road.

"Have you found the jewels?" she cried.

"We shall soon know." After spreading his black coat on the ground, Devlin opened the drawstring and turned the pouch upside down. Jane's breath caught as sparkling diamonds, glowing rubies and brilliant emeralds and sapphires tumbled onto the cloth.

After more than a century and a half, the Stuart Jewels had been found.

Sixteen

"The Stuart Jewels are found at last!" Devlin cried.

Grasping Jane's hands in his, he led her in a joyous dance, whirling her around and around and around.

Seeing Tommy's wistful look, Jane reached out and took one of the boy's hands. Devlin held the other and the three of them danced in a circle around the gleaming jewels. When they finally paused, breathless, Devlin let go of their hands and knelt to scoop the jewels into the pouch. Rising, he put one arm around Jane's shoulders and the other around Tommy's, drawing them to him, hugging them as though he would never let them go.

"I could not have found the jewels without your help," he said, "you, Jane and you, Tommy. I give both of you my profoundest thanks." As they smiled at him, he released them, adding belatedly, "I feel certain the Prince Regent will be equally grateful."

Stepping back, Jane said, "Yes, of course, you must return the jewels to the Prince." There was the slightest hint of a question in her voice.

"Without a moment's delay. I intend to leave this very morning for London." Devlin looked sharply at her. "Is there a reason I should not?" he asked.

She shook her head. "No reason, none at all. These are the king's jewels, there can be little doubt of that. They must be returned so he can add them to his collection in the Tower."

"Exactly." Again Devlin paused. "I note you use the word 'collection.' Are you, perhaps, thinking of our recent host, Squire Hopkins? You should realize, Jane, that there is no similarity whatsoever between the Crown Jewels of England and our Downland squire's hoard of snuffboxes."

She eyed him levelly. "I see no similarity, none at all. The jewels are the emblems of a great nation while the snuffboxes are the symbols of one man's foolishness."

"Must you keep saying 'none at all' when what you mean is just the opposite?" Devlin scowled. "You have a penchant, Jane, for taking a joyous occasion and changing it into one of gloom. Do you actually believe I should betray my trust and keep these jewels for myself? Or share them with you?"

She shook her head impatiently. Once more Devlin had failed to understand her meaning. Would he ever understand her?

"The jewels are England's," she said, "not yours or mine. I would never expect to receive nor would I accept money for helping bring about their safe return. I suppose I feel saddened to have them put to no practical use when I look around me and see so many children in need."

Tommy, whose gaze had shifted from Jane to Devlin and back to Jane again, said, "Stored them for the king, you did, for hundreds and hundreds of years. Ain't that worth something?"

Devlin stared at the boy, then picked him up and lifted him onto his shoulder. "The Bible tells us," he said with a smile, "that small pitchers have wide ears." Holding Tommy on his shoulder, he turned to Jane, seeming, for a moment, at a loss. Then he swung Tommy to the ground and said, stiffly, "Further discussion of the jewels will do more harm than good. I intend to leave for town with Tommy as soon as possible and once there I shall make haste to return the jewels to the Prince."

"As you should." Jane swallowed a sigh. She knew Devlin had no choice and yet, recalling the few weeks she had known him, that time a bittersweet mixture of happiness and regret, she felt as though he was deserting her. "Sometimes I wish—" she began.

"What is it you wish?" Devlin wanted to know.

She recognized the bite of anger in his voice and wondered whether some of that anger came from a feeling of guilt. Could it be that Devlin really sympathized with her, agreed with her at least in part about the jewels but still felt compelled by his sense of duty not to question his resolve to return them to the Prince? Or was there something more? A regret at leaving her? Or was she indulging in wishful thinking by hoping that she and Devlin thought alike?

"Jane," Devlin said, with no trace left of anger, "you seem to have gone into some sort of a trance. I asked what it was you wished."

"Sometimes I wish," she said softly, "that we could

begin again, you and I. Sometimes I wonder what would have happened if your carriage had truly lost a wheel, forcing you to seek refuge at Lyon Hall with no thought of discovering the secret of the King's Cloak or recovering the missing crown jewels."

Devlin shook his head. "A romantic notion," he said, "but a completely impractical one. The past is behind us, it cannot be relived, all we shall ever have is the present and the future."

His words brought a sting of tears to her eyes but she blinked them back and said tartly, "I never promised to be practical."

"The sooner the jewels are returned to their rightful owner," he told her, "not the Prince Regent but the English monarchy, the better it will be for both of us." He gazed at the pouch in his hand and frowned. "Perhaps Oliver Cromwell and his Roundheads put a curse on these jewels after they were spirited away from them, and your family has suffered ill-fortune because of that curse ever since. Whether they have or not, I hope you can view things more clearly, Jane, once the jewels are safely back in the Tower."

"I hope so," she said, not trying to keep the wistful sadness from her voice.

Devlin was obviously anxious to return the jewels and to leave Lyon Hall. To leave her? She lifted her chin, determined to neither say nor do anything to try to make him change his mind. Pride might afford cold comfort but it was all she had.

Devlin started to reply but, evidently thinking better of it, said nothing. After retrieving his coat from the

ground, he lifted Tommy into the curricle, handed Jane
to a seat beside the boy and they drove back to the
Hall in an oppressive silence.

Devlin and Tommy were ready to leave Lyon Hall
less than an hour later, intending, she knew, to return
the curricle to Lord Lansdowne and then go on to London in Devlin's landau.

Though Devlin raised Jane's hand to his lips and
though he bade her a pleasant enough farewell, promising to return as soon as his business in town was
finished, she felt his words and gestures to be perfunctory, the leave-taking expected of a gentleman of the
ton. Lord Devlin, she reminded herself, would always
behave like a gentleman as well as a loyal servant of
the Crown.

She wished Devlin and Tommy godspeed; she
watched them, watched Devlin rather, until the curricle
was out of sight, wondering all the while if she would
see him ever again. When she turned away to go back
into the Hall, she did her best to swallow the lump in
her throat but it persisted along with the melancholy
knowledge that if Devlin did come back it might only
be to fetch Horatio from the Lyon Hall stables.

Should she have been so cool and aloof toward
him? Should she have tried to suppress her anger and
her disappointment and confess her love for him?
Would she always regret that she had clung to her
pride rather than admit the depth of her feelings? But
she had not revealed how she felt, the moment had
passed and, as Devlin had reminded her, would never
return. The past was gone, she had only the present

and future. She would put him from her thoughts until he returned for Horatio. Even then, she would try her best to avoid him. There was more to life than Lord Devlin.

Her resolve to put him from her thoughts, however, proved impossible to keep. In her mind, the days that followed became the days without Devlin.

On the first day without Devlin she struggled with the estate books but the final totals, no matter how computed, always proved disheartening.

On the second day without Devlin, Estelle—Jane had told her of the recovery of the cloak from LaSalle and the discovery of the jewels—showed her an item in the *Gazette:*

MYSTERIOUS AFFAIR AT ARUNDEL
BALLOON ABANDONED

Our special correspondent in West Sussex reports that a damaged balloon was discovered on the farm of Mr. Joseph Hunter of Arundel following the recent storm. The origin of the balloon and its occupants, if any, remain a mystery.

Harry Funnell, a local shepherd, told our correspondent that he observed a stranger, a man who walked with a limp, leaving the area on foot. This stranger, Funnell suspected, was a foreigner, possibly a Frenchman. . . .

Jane gave a sigh of relief. "Thank goodness," she said to Estelle, "M. LaSalle appears to be safe." Thief

though he had proved to be, she could not find it in
her heart to wish him ill.

On the third day without Devlin, a blustery Decem-
ber day, Jane tried to pass the time by starting one of
Estelle's circulating library novels but soon found herself finishing a page with not the slightest notion of
what she had just read. Again and again her thoughts
returned to Devlin. She relived their time together at
the Angel Inn, once again feeling the thrill of being
in his arms. Recalling their picnic at the Lansdowne
Folly, she sighed, wondering if she would ever be that
happy again.

On the fourth day without Devlin, Jane and Estelle
drove to Midhurst for shopping followed by tea at the
Spread Eagle Inn. On their return to Lyon Hall, they
were met by Joshua, the stable boy, who led them into
the barn to see what he called "a sight to behold."
There, in the corner of an empty stall, Chatter lay
curled beside Horatio. Both animals were asleep.

Surprised beyond measure, Jane could only stand
and stare.

Chatter opened his eyes, gave Jane a haughty look
as if to remind her that what he did was his own affair,
and then closed them again.

"They say the day will come," Estelle said, "when
the lamb shall lie with the lion. Still, I admit to being
astonished."

Jane recalled Chatter's fear of Horatio on the night
of Devlin's arrival. Now, however, the two had apparently decided to accept one another. Could this unex-

pected harmony between cat and dog be a good omen? she wondered.

On the fifth day without Devlin, another blustering day and night of wind and rain, Jane waited until the house slept before returning to the drawing room to work on her estate ledger. After but a short time, she shook her head in resignation.

"Impossible," she said to Chatter. The cat, who was settled comfortably on a cushion on one of the chairs by the fire, paid her no heed, not even bothering to open his eyes.

The Tompion clock on the mantel chimed once and was silent; the single candle on Jane's writing desk flared and then flickered as it burned low in its socket; the embers in the fireplace winked out one by one until only a few remained. The dark chill of the night seemed to have crept into the Lyon Hall where now it lurked in all the shadowed corners of the room.

Jane recalled another night of wind and rain, a night when she had defiantly lit candles in all the drawing room windows, a night when a knocking at the door had announced the arrival of a stranger seeking refuge from the storm. She sighed, reminding herself the past was just that, past. The present, though, held little hope for happiness and she dreaded what the future might bring.

A loud knocking echoed through the house, once, twice, three times, startling Jane from her melancholy reverie. Her heart leaped. Could it be Devlin returning from London? But that was highly unlikely at this time of night.

Jane, knowing Hendricks had retired for the night, walked into the entry hall and opened the front door a crack. As she peered into the darkness, she breathed in the damp cold of the night and heard the pattering of the rain on the graveled sweep. A tall figure emerged from out of the gloom.

"Devlin!" she cried, flinging the door wide as joy leaped within her. How handsome he was! And how wonderful to see him.

"My carriage," he told her, "suffered an unexpected mishap on the Midhurst Road, a lost wheel to be precise, and so I come here to beg refuge for the night."

Puzzled, she stared at him, her smile fading. And then, suddenly, she realized what he was about, that he was complying with her wish that they could begin again. "Come in, Lord Devlin," she said, stepping to one side, "and welcome to Lyon Hall."

"Capital." Devlin entered, removed his greatcoat and tossed it onto a chair.

"This way, my lord," she said, leading him along the hall to the drawing room, anticipation mixing with uncertainty. Though she understood what he was doing, she was unsure why.

After bowing to her, he strode across the room to the hearth where he held his hands to the few glowing embers. Turning to her, he said, "You are, I believe, an American."

"I am."

"Your hair, I note," he said, "is a wonderful shade of red and your eyes are a quite remarkable green."

"No, my hair happens to be auburn, my eyes are

hazel." She found herself breathless, scarcely able to
utter the words she remembered using when first they
met.

"Ah, yes," he said, "quite right, I confess I was mistaken, as I have been about many things." He glanced
around the room, first at Chatter on his chair and then
toward the archway leading to the King's Room. "I was
given to understand," he said, "that you have a cloak at
Lyon Hall, a blue velvet cloak dating from the time of
Charles I."

"The King's Cloak," she said, gesturing toward the
King's Room, "has been on display here at Lyon Hall
for many years. I will, if you wish, be most happy to
show it to you."

Devlin shook his head. "There are those in London
who claim the cloak contains a secret, a clue to the
whereabouts of the so-called Stuart Jewels. I, however,
have no interest in cloaks or jewels."

And why should he, she asked herself, now that he
had delivered them to the Prince. Her expectations of
being able to change the past faded away. "Enough of
your charade, Devlin," she said. "Pray tell me what
happened in London."

"I assure you it is not a charade," he insisted. "You
asked to begin again; I was merely making your wish
come true." When she started to speak, he held up his
hand and said, "But before I go on, I *will* tell you
what occurred after Tommy and I arrived in London.
On the third day of my visit I was honored by being
summoned into the presence of the Prince Regent himself."

"At Carlton House?"

"Yes, I was privileged to have a very private audience with the Prince at Carlton House." Devlin smiled. "The Prince was most gracious to me but of course he would be since he was well aware of the purpose of my visit. He is, by the bye, becoming every bit as plump as a Christmas goose."

"You gave him the jewels, I expect," she said, wanting him to finish his tale and have done with it.

"The Prince proved to be outrageously flattering," Devlin went on without answering her. "He praised my perseverance in the search for the jewels, he lauded what he referred to as my cleverness and he applauded my steadfast loyalty to the Crown. He also thanked me for my many services to the throne and hinted at honors that would soon come my way."

Jane nodded as she listened for she knew that Devlin *did* possess all of those admirable traits. He also, she suspected, had been vastly pleased by the royal flattery—as who would not be?—even though now he appeared to make light of it.

"The Prince proceeded to take me into his confidence," Devlin said, "regaling me with a new and wondrous scheme of his, a plan to employ John Nash to expand the pavilion by the sea at Brighton into a marvelous structure in the Oriental mode with a multitude of exotic domes and towers. When finished, the Prince assured me, the pavilion will be the eighth wonder of the world."

Jane's heart sank. Devlin was telling her that the Stuart Jewels would be exchanged for another pile of stones built in the grand manner, another Folly, this time a royal Folly. But then, had she not expected just such a possibility?

"After leaving the Prince and returning to my town house," Devlin said, "I made two rather amazing discoveries. To my everlasting amazement and without a doubt owing to my excitement stemming from the Prince's flattering attention, I found I had overlooked something." He reached into the pocket of his waistcoat, brought forth a small velvet case and, with a flourish, opened it.

Speechless, Jane stared down at three large diamonds sparkling in their nests of black velvet.

"I had neglected," Devlin said, "to give these three jewels to the Prince when I gave him the others."

Jane gazed from the diamonds to Devlin, completely at sea.

"The Prince shall have his pavilion at Brighton," Devlin said, "but at the same time we, you and I, shall do something for deserving lads such as Tommy Boggs and Joshua. We shall start a school, perhaps here at Lyon Hall, perhaps in London. If we decide to convert Lyon Hall into a school and Estelle desires to live elsewhere, with my Aunt Charlotte's help—I left Tommy with Lottie, by the bye—I could easily make a place for Estelle in London. I believe she prefers the excitement of the town to the more placid joys of the country."

"A school," Jane said slowly, her head awhirl. She had never dreamed Devlin would be so bold. Unless she had heard wrong, they were both to be involved in the school. What might that imply?

"Not my idea, Jane, I take pleasure in giving you full credit." He smiled. "Now for the second and probably more important discovery I made while in London. Do you recollect my telling you once, I believe it was while both of us were guests at the infamous Angel Inn, of the day my father took me to meet the Prince's father, King George III, and how ever afterwards I believed something extraordinary would one day happen to me?"

"I remember very well." That conversation was not all she recalled of their time together on their journey north to London. How could she ever forget the wonder of Devlin's kisses? "I suppose," she said, "you decided that your private audience with the Prince was that extraordinary event."

"Jane, you are often right in your supposes, but in this case you happen to be completely and totally mistaken."

Devlin took her hand in his, leading her to the settee where he sat beside her. "I always believed," he said, "that I would recognize the unusual destiny I expected was in store for me at the very moment it occurred. On thinking back over my audience with the Prince and after a few moments of reflection, however, I realized how wrong this notion was, realized that extraordinary happenings do not necessarily strike one like a bolt of lightning from an unclouded sky. They often occur without one being aware of their significance at the time."

"Many good things take years to mature and develop," she said. "As a child slowly but surely grows to become an adult."

"Or a love grows," he said, bringing her fingers to his lips in a gentle caress.

Jane gazed bemusedly at Devlin, warmed by his touch, thrilled by his words, eager with anticipation yet fearing she had misconstrued his meaning.

"The extraordinary thing—rather the sequence of extraordinary things that happened to me," Devlin said, "began when first I came to Lyon Hall in search of the King's Cloak. Ever since then, whilst I was frantically seeking first the cloak and then the Stuart Jewels, without realizing what was happening, I found myself slowly but surely becoming aware of something far more valuable than either cloak or jewels."

He paused and raised his hand to gently touch her cheek. "You, Jane," he said, "are a jewel worth a great deal more than the diamonds or the rubies or the emeralds or the sapphires I gave to the Prince Regent."

Devlin reached hesitantly into his pocket. "This," he told her, "is a letter to you that I composed tonight on my way to Lyon Hall. Because the message is for you and you alone, I took the precaution of putting it in code."

What a strange thing to do, she thought. But then Devlin rarely seemed to do the expected. He would, she hoped, never change.

He seemed somewhat nervous as he handed her a folded piece of paper. Wondering why, she opened the paper and peered down at the jumble of letters:

"I OVEL UOY," she read, frowning at words that at first glance made no sense. "ILLW UOY ARRYM EM?"

Then the meaning of the message sprang out at her. "Oh, Devlin," she cried, half laughing, half crying. "I do love you and I will marry you, of course I will. How could you ever doubt it?"

He gathered her into his arms and, when he kissed her, she knew she had found her home at last.

ZEBRA'S REGENCY ROMANCES
DAZZLE AND DELIGHT

A BEGUILING INTRIGUE (4441, $3.99)
by Olivia Sumner

Pretty as a picture Justine Riggs cared nothing for propriety. She dressed as a boy, sat on her horse like a jockey, and pondered the stars like a scientist. But when she tried to best the handsome Quenton Fletcher, Marquess of Devon, by proving that she was the better equestrian, he would try to prove Justine's antics were pure folly. The game he had in mind was seduction — never imagining that he might lose his heart in the process!

AN INCONVENIENT ENGAGEMENT (4442, $3.99)
by Joy Reed

Rebecca Wentworth was furious when she saw her betrothed waltzing with another. So she decides to make him jealous by flirting with the handsomest man at the ball, John Collinwood, Earl of Stanford. The "wicked" nobleman knew exactly what the enticing miss was up to — and he was only too happy to play along. But as Rebecca gazed into his magnificent eyes, her errant fiancé was soon utterly forgotten!

SCANDAL'S LADY (4472, $3.99)
by Mary Kingsley

Cassandra was shocked to learn that the new Earl of Lynton was her childhood friend, Nicholas St. John. After years at sea and mixed feelings Nicholas had come home to take the family title. And although Cassandra knew her place as a governess, she could not help the thrill that went through her each time he was near. Nicholas was pleased to find that his old friend Cassandra was his new next door neighbor, but after being near her, he wondered if mere friendship would be enough . . .

HIS LORDSHIP'S REWARD (4473, $3.99)
by Carola Dunn

As the daughter of a seasoned soldier, Fanny Ingram was accustomed to the vagaries of military life and cared not a whit about matters of rank and social standing. So she certainly never foresaw her *tendre* for handsome Viscount Roworth of Kent with whom she was forced to share lodgings, while he carried out his clandestine activities on behalf of the British Army. And though good sense told Roworth to keep his distance, he couldn't stop from taking Fanny in his arms for a kiss that made all hearts equal!